Nightmare Ride

Max was cantering Popsicle down one long side of the big outdoor ring, which at the moment seemed to go on forever. He was supposed to jump a big stone wall at the far end of the ring, but Popsicle's canter never brought him any closer to the jump. . . . The closer he came to the stone wall, the larger it grew. *How are we ever going to clear that?* he thought frantically. He wanted to pull up, but it was too late. . . . Then he was at the fence. . . . Popsicle tried to jump the wall. They went up, up, nearly to the top, then, horribly, they began to fall. Max looked down and saw the mud below. Popsicle would surely break a leg. Max had made a terrible mistake! He shouldn't have tried to jump that fence; he should have known it was just too high. He tried to urge Popsicle upward again, but it was no use. The clouds whirled overhead as he and the horse fell and fell toward the ground.

Books in the SHORT STIRRUP CLUB™ series
(by Allison Estes)

#1 Blue Ribbon Friends
#2 Ghost of Thistle Ridge
#3 The Great Gymkhana Gamble

Available from MINSTREL BOOKS

The Great Gymkhana Gamble

Allison Estes

Published by POCKET BOOKS
New York London Toronto Sydney Tokyo Singapore

A MINSTREL PAPERBACK *Original*

A Minstrel Book published by
POCKET BOOKS, a division of Simon & Schuster Inc.
1230 Avenue of the Americas, New York, NY 10020

ISBN: 0-671-54518-3

First Minstrel Books printing August 1996

10 9 8 7 6 5 4 3 2 1

Cover photo by Pat Hill; shot on location at Overpeck Riding Academy, New Jersey

Printed in the U.S.A.

To all the beloved teachers, especially Linda Jordan, Anna Clark, Miss Murchison, Willie Morris, and Ms. Douglass, who gave me the structure of language and the freedom to create with it, I dedicate this book with thanks.

"Short Stirrup" is a division in horse shows, open to riders age twelve and under. Additional requirements may vary from show to show.

The Great Gymkhana Gamble

1

MAX MORRISON RODE PAST THE GATE, SAT BACK, AND asked his horse to halt. His ten-year-old chestnut gelding, Popsicle, stopped perfectly square and lowered his head. Max sat for a count of five and then asked Popsicle to walk on, letting him stretch his head down and pull the reins through his fingers. He leaned forward and gave the horse a big, satisfied pat on his shiny, reddish-brown neck.

"Good boy," he said approvingly.

Max's twin sister, Megan, trotted up on her dapple-gray pony, Pixie. She began to walk alongside Max and Popsicle as they circled the big outdoor ring.

"Gosh, Max, is that all you're going to do?"

Megan asked. "You've been practicing halting forever. Don't you want to canter or something?"

Max looked at his sister, whose face was flushed from the hot summer sun. Her brown eyes sparkled, hinting at her mischievous nature.

"I'll race you around the arena!" she challenged him. "Come on, I'll give you a head start." She impatiently pushed a lock of her wavy brown hair back under her safety helmet and waited for Max to answer.

Max shook his head. "No thanks. Besides, you always win. You know Pixie's faster than Popsicle."

"I'm not so sure she's faster. It's just that you never give Popsicle a chance. I think you always hold him back." Megan said. "Come on, let him go, Max. I dare you!" Pixie began to prance as she felt her young rider take up the reins.

"I do not hold him back," Max said defensively. "Pixie's just faster." But he couldn't quite look his sister in the eye. He leaned over and pretended to be very busy placing a stirrup under his foot. "We're not supposed to be racing, anyway," he added, straightening up. "You know it's dangerous." His blue-gray eyes were serious.

Megan let out an impatient sigh and trotted away from her brother. Max watched as his sister cantered, then bent forward and urged her pony into a controlled hand gallop, racing herself around the ring. It looked like fun. For a moment, he considered joining her. She had been right about his holding Popsicle back. He had never let his horse go all out, even though Popsicle was a quarter horse, bred to be as fast as a thoroughbred for a quarter of a mile. Max was pretty sure if he ever did let Popsicle go, he could beat her. Megan's pony was quick, but she was only a pony. He just didn't think he could let Popsicle go that fast, though. What if the horse tripped, or pulled a muscle, or even broke a leg?

Suddenly, Max was irritated with his sister. Megan had a knack for making the craziest ideas sound perfectly reasonable. She was always challenging him to do things they weren't really supposed to be doing. Impulsively, he pressed Popsicle forward into the track, where he would block Megan's path as she galloped around the ring. She had to slow down to avoid running into him. Pixie tossed up her head in annoyance.

"Ma-ax! Cut it out!" Megan said.

"You cut it out," Max told her sternly. "You're not supposed to be galloping, anyway."

"Oh, shush," Megan retorted.

"Anyway, Pixie's hot. You ought to be walking her out."

"She's not that hot." Megan tossed her head the same way her pony just had. "Anyway, Popsicle's sweaty, too, and all you've been doing is standing around."

"I have not been standing around. I've been practicing trot-to-halt transitions like Sharon told me to." Sharon Wyndham was Max and Megan's trainer. She and her husband, Jake, owned the more than one hundred seventy acres of hilly woods and pastures that made up Thistle Ridge Farm.

Max gazed out at the rolling hills as he spoke. He was thinking of the first time he'd seen Thistle Ridge. Earlier in the summer, the Morrisons had moved from Connecticut to Hickoryville, Tennessee, a little town just outside Memphis. The twins' mother, Dr. Rose Morrison, had been hired as head of orthopedics at the big, new medical center there. James Morrison, the twins' father, was a famous artist. Max remembered how angry he'd been at his parents for making them move. He'd hated leaving their old barn in Connecticut. Now he could hardly imagine being anywhere else.

Thistle Ridge Farm had come to seem more like a home to Max than a barn. He and Megan spent every moment they could at the stables, riding or brushing their horses or picking out their stalls. Sometimes they rambled across the pastures or watched the farrier at work shoeing horses. Often they watched the lessons going on in the spacious arenas. But most of all, they looked forward to their own weekly lessons with Sharon Wyndham.

Although Max had loved his old trainer back in Connecticut, he thought Sharon Wyndham was the best teacher he'd ever had. Sharon had ridden for the United States Equestrian Team in the last Olympics, bringing home a gold and a bronze medal. She was preparing now for the next Olympics, which would be held in Atlanta, Georgia.

Max wanted to go and see Sharon ride more than anything. Atlanta wasn't far away, but it would be a very expensive trip. His parents had told him they would help him get there if he earned the money to pay for the tickets himself. Max was determined to earn the money somehow—but so far, he hadn't figured out how an eleven-year-old could earn more than a hundred dollars.

Max swayed in the saddle as Popsicle took a few steps forward. He had almost forgotten that he was sitting on his horse in one of the outdoor rings at Thistle Ridge Farm. He was thinking about how exciting it would be to watch Sharon ride at the Olympics.

Sharon had two big Dutch warmblood horses, Quasar and Cuckabur, who were spending the summer at Thistle Ridge. After a busy season of traveling to horse shows, Sharon always gave her horses a few months off. Max had become especially fond of Quasar, Sharon's big dressage horse.

Although Max and Megan had always shown in hunter-jumper divisions in the local horse shows, lately Max had taken an interest in dressage. Megan was always saying that dressage was just "for stuffy old ladies who are too scared to jump." Until now, Max had always agreed with her. At their old barn, almost no one did dressage. But at Thistle Ridge, lots of people did. There was even a whole ring just for dressage riders. Max had been watching them a lot lately.

To Megan, dressage was just "slow." She'd dismissed it as "about as exciting as a turtle race." But Max was finding dressage more and more interesting. He'd learned that what looked slow to his sister was really *collection*—skilled riders asking their horses to carry most of their weight on their hindquarters, so that they could perform complex moves forward, sideways, and even in place. Max admired the precision necessary in a dressage test, where the riders had to carry out certain moves at specific places in the ring.

A few times, he had watched Sharon practicing on Quasar. When collected, the big warmblood seemed to dance around the arena, his white-stockinged legs flashing. When Sharon asked the horse to lengthen his stride, he flung out his front legs and sailed across the ring in an extended trot, hardly seeming to touch the ground. Max had been awed by the graceful power of the big chestnut and the quiet strength of Sharon's riding.

He had tried to tell his sister about it, but Megan never seemed interested. She only wanted to know how high they had jumped. It had made Max realize that he and his twin really were very different, not just in looks. Max was tall and slim like his mother, with the same light hair and eyes. Megan had inherited her father's coloring and sturdy build. People were always surprised to find out that Megan and Max were twins. Max was surprised himself sometimes.

Their lessons with Sharon were a perfect example. Megan was always hard on herself when things didn't go well with Pixie in a lesson, but she seldom worked on the problems on her own time. When the lesson was over, she went right back to just bombing around on her pony. If she did well in a lesson or a show, she was happy about it. If she didn't, she never thought about it much afterward.

Max was just the opposite. He always rode carefully and thoughtfully. Judges at horse shows loved the team of Max and Popsicle cantering quietly around a big, grassy hunter course, effortlessly clearing the natural fences. Max usually did well at shows and in his lessons, because he worked hard at it, practicing carefully between lessons, as he had been doing today. When Megan did well, she always said she was just lucky. When Max put in a good round, it was because he practiced and it showed.

"Hey, Max!" a familiar voice called out.

Max turned and waved when he saw Keith Hill coming toward the arena leading his quarter-horse mare, Penny. Keith, who was ten years old, was Max's very best friend at Thistle Ridge. He had longish black hair, which he sometimes wore in a ponytail. Like his mother, who was a Native American, Keith had very dark tan skin. Both of his parents were teachers at the university in Memphis.

Keith's horse whinnied happily when she saw Popsicle, and even pranced for a stride or two before she remembered her manners. Popsicle called back to Penny as he usually did and waited with his ears pricked forward as they entered the arena.

Keith led Penny to the center of the ring, where Max sat on Popsicle. The two horses sniffed at each other and blew air into each other's nostrils. They were almost identical, except that Popsicle had one blue eye. The only other way to tell them apart was by their tack; Max rode English, while Penny wore a western saddle and bridle. Keith grabbed the saddle horn and struggled to get his left foot up high enough to put it into the stirrup so he could mount up.

"I hope you tightened your cinch this time," Max said to him. Keith was always falling off Penny when the saddle slid to the side because he'd failed to get the cinch tight enough.

"I hope I did, too." Keith laughed. "Or else, I hope she's still puffing her belly out." He stuck his foot in the stirrup and managed to swing his other leg over without the saddle slipping. "Made it! How's Popsicle today?" he asked Max.

"Good." Max scratched Popsicle on his withers just above his shoulder and in front of the saddle. Popsicle closed his eyes and gave a little groan of pleasure. "We've been practicing our trot-to-halt transitions."

Keith nodded. "I've got to practice my turns today. I'm going to a western show Saturday."

"What are you showing in?" Max asked curiously. He'd never been to a Western horse show.

"Western equitation, where they judge the rider, and pleasure, where they judge the horse. And barrel racing, of course. That's my favorite event, and Penny's too!" He patted Penny's neck enthusiastically. "Right, ol' girl?"

"Did somebody say 'racing'?" Megan said as she trotted over to the boys.

Keith nodded. "Barrel racing. I've got a show this Saturday."

"I've always wanted to try barrel racing." Megan said. "It's too bad they don't have events like that in English horse shows." Her face lit up as she had an idea. "Hey, can you be in a Western show and ride in English tack?" she asked.

Keith thought about it. "I don't think so. I think you have to show in Western tack at a Western show, unless it's an English pleasure class. Sometimes they have those at Western shows."

"Well, I don't see why it matters," Megan frowned. "As long as you get around the barrels fast, why should they care what kind of saddle your pony is wearing?"

"In Western, you neck-rein. You have to hold the reins in one hand. To steer, you shift your hand, and the horse turns when he feels the rein touch his neck. It wouldn't be fair for one rider to be using two hands to steer with a direct rein like you do in English," Keith explained. "Besides, there are lots of events where you have to use your free hand to close gates and things like that. If you were riding English, you'd have some trouble with that since you have to use both hands to steer."

"Not me," Megan said. "I can do anything with the reins in one hand that I can do with them in two. Watch!"

Max and Keith watched as Megan shortened her reins and put them into one hand. She put her other hand behind her back. Then she picked up a trot, rode a curvy, serpentine pattern up one side of the ring, halted, backed up, cantered a circle, then asked Pixie to change her leading leg and cantered in the other direction. With one hand still behind her back, she came down to a trot, trotted a circle around Max and Keith, and finally halted on Max's right side, so that she was abreast of Popsicle and Penny.

"See?" Megan said, panting. She stuck her free hand up in a gesture of triumph, then reached forward and patted Pixie's dappled neck. "Now, where are those barrels? Let me at 'em!"

"Show-off," Max muttered.

"That's pretty good," Keith said to Megan. "Can you jump like that, with your reins in one hand?"

"I can jump with no hands at all," Megan said smugly. "Want to see?"

"No way," Max said firmly. "Remember what happened the last time you jumped when you weren't supposed to, Megan?" He gave her a warning look.

There were lots of deer roaming the woods and pastures at Thistle Ridge Farm. Pixie had been terrified of them at first. One day, Megan had jumped Pixie over a fence in the back pasture and startled a deer out of its hiding place in the woods nearby. Pixie was so spooked that she bolted for the barn, completely out of control. Megan was lucky that neither she nor Pixie had been hurt.

"Well, anyway, I *can* do it," Megan grumbled.

"You can do what?" said a friendly voice.

Max, Keith, and Megan waved at Chloe Goodman, who had come down the path from the barn while they were talking. Chloe was twelve, just a little older than Max and Megan, but she was small for her age. She and Megan were nearly inseparable. Max liked Chloe very much, too. It was hard not to—she was helpful around the barn and kind to everybody. Chloe did barn chores in return for her lessons and the board on her pony, Jump for Joy.

Jump for Joy was a beautiful, fancy white pony that had once belonged to Amanda Sloane. Max couldn't help making a face when he thought of Amanda. She was snobbish and mean to everyone. But Chloe was even nice to Amanda Sloane!

"How's Jump for Joy today?" Megan called out to her friend.

"Oh, about the same, I guess." Chloe's expression turned sad. "I feel so sorry for him, having to just stand in his stall like that for so long."

Jump for Joy was recovering from a torn ligament in his right front leg. It had happened when Amanda rode him recklessly through the mud at the last horse show. Everyone feared that the pony's leg was broken. Max still shuddered every time he thought of it. He'd been standing at the rail watching the class when the accident happened. Now, every time he had to ride in mud, he felt extra anxious. What if something like that happened to Popsicle?

"How much longer is Jump for Joy on stall rest?" Max asked with concern.

"Well, Dr. Pepper is coming out in a few weeks to check him. If the tear is closed up, then he can start getting out some," Chloe explained. "I'll be so glad for him! I know he misses getting turned out."

"The poor guy," Max said sympathetically. He patted his own horse.

Jump for Joy had been a Pony Hunter champion many times. Amanda Sloane had been lucky to have him. Max grew angry every time he thought of how Amanda had been so careless with the pony. He was glad Chloe had ended up with him. The Sloanes had signed him over to her for nothing, just so they wouldn't have to pay the vet bills and board on him while he was recovering.

"What's that?" Megan asked Chloe. She pointed to the book Chloe had tucked under her arm. "I hope it's a book about how to raise money if you want to go to the Olympics." Megan, Chloe, and Keith were hoping to go to the Olympics just as much as Max was.

"Nope. Sorry. It's a book about gymkhanas. I've been reading all about them," Chloe said. She had only started riding that spring, but, like the other three kids, she loved it more than anything. She was always carrying around a book about horses or riding.

"A jim-who's-it?" Megan asked.

"Gymkhana." Chloe laughed. "It's a kind of horse show where they have games instead of equitation or just walk-trot-canter stuff. It sounds really fun."

"You mean like team games?" Keith asked.

"Yes," Chloe told him. "There are some individual events, too, but the team games sound like the most fun. Here, listen . . ."

The three children on horseback gathered around her. Chloe began reading them descriptions of some of the gymkhana games. Max wasn't really paying attention. He had begun daydreaming about the Olympics again.

"You guys!" Megan interrupted Chloe's reading. "I have a terrific idea. Let's have one."

"One what?" Max asked.

"A gymkhana!" Megan exclaimed. "Let's have a gymkhana to raise the money for the Olympic tickets!"

2

"WELL?" MEGAN ASKED. "WHAT DO YOU THINK?"

"I think a gymkhana's a great idea!" Keith said enthusiastically.

Chloe looked up at all of them. "It really does sound like fun," she agreed. "And it would be a good way to raise money for the Olympic tickets. Max, what do you think?"

Max hesitated. He wasn't at all sure he liked the idea. It sounded dangerous dashing around with lots of other horses, handing off batons and steering around obstacles. When he was cantering around a jump course or practicing transitions, Max felt confident about his riding. He even enjoyed trail riding all over Thistle Ridge Farm with

Keith. But he'd never done anything like the games Chloe had described. He wasn't sure he'd be good at them. What if he was terrible at mounted games?

"Well, Max?" Megan demanded. "The Short Stirrup Club awaits your vote. Do you want to have a gymkhana?"

Max looked around. Everyone was waiting for him to answer. Keith's dark eyes had a questioning look in them. In another second, Megan would start calling him a chicken. Max didn't want them to think that he was afraid, so he shrugged carelessly. "Sure," he managed to say. "Sounds . . . interesting."

"Great!" Megan exclaimed. "Now we just have to practice!"

"First we have to plan it," Chloe reminded her.

"First you have to get Sharon and Jake to agree to let us *have* the gymkhana," Max pointed out. He hoped they'd say no. Then he wouldn't have to worry about whether or not he'd be good at the games.

"Oops. I guess you're right," Megan said. "Well, what are we waiting for? Let's go find Jake!" She slid off Pixie and began running up the stirrups and loosening the girth.

"Jake went to town to pick up something," Keith told her.

"Oh." Megan paused. Max knew what she was thinking: Should they go ahead and ask Sharon about the gymkhana? They all loved Sharon but were a little in awe of her. Sharon liked everything done a certain way. Jake was much more easygoing. If they got Jake to agree first, Sharon was much more likely to say they could have the gymkhana.

"We could wait for Jake to come back," Chloe suggested.

"I can't go up yet, anyway," Keith said. "I still have to exercise Penny."

"I know!" Megan said excitedly. "Let's practice some of the games while we're waiting for Jake to get back."

"Great idea," Keith said. "What should we do?"

"Chloe, you read us the instructions for a game that sounds fun, and we'll try the hardest part of it," Megan said, pulling down her stirrups and preparing to mount up again.

"Okay," said Chloe, studying the book. "Here's one . . ." Chloe explained one of the relay races which involved handing off a baton.

"Hey, Max," Keith said, "want to try a handoff?"

"Sure," said Max, trying to sound enthusiastic, though he didn't feel that way at all. "What'll we use for a baton?"

They looked around. "How about your bat?"

Megan pointed to the short bat Max carried. Popsicle was a very laid-back horse; sometimes it took a little smack behind Max's leg to get him going.

"That'll do," Chloe said. "It says here that the use of whips or spurs in mounted games is strictly forbidden. You might as well use your bat for a baton, Max, since you won't be using it in the gymkhana. Megan, you'll have to drop yours, too."

"Here you go." Megan tossed her bat to Chloe. At the same moment, Max walked Popsicle forward to avoid a fly that had been nagging him. Megan's bat hit Popsicle right in the rump!

The startled horse scooted forward. Max was nearly left behind, but he managed to lean forward and stay with the motion. He quickly shortened the reins and stopped Popsicle. He turned to face his sister.

"Oops!" She giggled. "Sorry, Max."

Max wasn't laughing at all. He had almost fallen off Popsicle. His heart his thumping as he said angrily. "What's the matter with you, Megan? Are you trying to kill me?"

Megan did her best to keep a straight face. "I'm sorry, Max, really I am. I was just tossing my bat to Chloe. I didn't know you were going to cross in front of me right then. You know I didn't mean for it to hit Popsicle."

"Well, you're not supposed to throw your bat at

all! You don't throw things around horses! What if I had fallen off?" Max demanded.

"Oh, come on, Max, get over it." Megan rolled her eyes. "I said I'm sorry."

"Sorry doesn't help," Max muttered. He patted Popsicle's neck as if to soothe him, but Popsicle seemed to have forgotten the incident already. He stood peacefully, his eyes half-closed, gently swishing his tail from side to side.

"Let's try the game," Keith said. "Who wants to be first?"

"I do," said Megan. "We can start back there by the gate. We'll ride up to the other end, around the little stone-wall jump, and back. I'll hand off to you, Keith, and you hand off to Grouchy over there." She motioned toward Max. He made a face at her, so Megan stuck out her tongue.

"I'll say go," Chloe offered.

The three rode down toward the gate and turned to face the opposite end of the arena.

"Ready?" Chloe called.

"I'm ready," Megan said, grasping the baton.

Chloe yelled out, "On your mark, get set . . . GO!"

Megan pushed her legs into Pixie's sides and cantered off toward the far end. Max watched as she turned quickly around the little jump and came thundering back, holding out the baton to Keith. He grabbed it, kicked at Penny's sides, and off they went. The old mare galloped up the side of the arena like a three-year-old, turned neatly around the jump, and galloped back.

Max waited nervously as they charged toward him. The closer Keith got, the more uncomfortable Max felt. Then Keith was next to him, reaching out with the baton. But he waved it right in Popsicle's face!

Popsicle shied sideways. Keith leaned out farther, trying to give Max the baton. The next thing Max knew, Keith had landed in the dirt with a thud. The cinch on Penny's saddle was too loose again!

"Ouch!" Keith howled. "Shoot!"

"Keith, are you okay?" Chloe ran to help him up.

"Yeah, I'm fine," Keith said. He got up slowly, trying to smile as he wiped tears from his eyes. "Boy, that really hurt."

"Are you sure you're okay?" Max was concerned for his friend. He'd seen Keith fall off half a dozen times since he'd known him, usually because Penny's saddle slid to the side as it had just done. But Keith usually laughed it off and climbed back on right away. This time, he was definitely not laughing.

"Boy, that was a hard one." Keith shook his head. He was standing with one hand on his hip. "I'll be fine," he said in a shaky voice as he limped toward his horse. Penny stood patiently waiting for someone to fix the saddle, which hung off her right side. Max didn't think Keith looked fine at all. He could see his friend wincing every time he moved his right leg.

When Keith had the saddle on straight again, he prepared to mount up. But when he went to put his left foot into the stirrup, he had to take it out again because his other leg hurt too much. He stood still, a surprised look on his face.

"Do you need help, Keith?" Chloe hurried to his side. Max looked on anxiously.

Keith slowly shook his head. "I'll get back on in a little bit. Maybe my hip just needs a rest." He took Penny's reins and led her out of the ring. The others watched him limp up the hill toward the barn.

"Well, the two of us could practice," Megan suggested to her brother.

Max gave his sister a scornful look. "You never know when it's time to quit, do you, Megan?"

"As far as I'm concerned, there's never a time to be a *quitter,*" Megan retorted.

Max dismounted and ran up his stirrups. "Keith's really hurt, Megan. I'm going to make sure he's all right." He loosened Popsicle's girth. "You go on and practice all you want. By yourself." He took the reins over Popsicle's head and led him out of the arena. He closed the gate behind him, giving his sister a disgusted look.

"What's the matter with him?" he heard Megan say to Chloe as he started up the hill.

What is the matter with me? Max wondered. Lately he'd begun to feel nervous every time he rode. It didn't have anything to do with Popsicle, Max knew. He scratched his horse on the neck as he led him into the barn. Popsicle was just about perfect. He almost never misbehaved. So what was it? Max couldn't be sure. He just knew that every time he rode, the nervous feeling seemed to get worse. He'd begun to spend a little less time riding because of it. And then there was the dream . . . He quickly dismissed the thought of it. *Maybe I just need a little break from riding* he told himself.

He untacked Popsicle and put him in his stall, planning to brush him later. First he wanted to find Keith. Penny was in her stall, but Max didn't see Keith anywhere. He went down the side aisle and looked in the wash stalls. Keith wasn't there. Then he went into the courtyard and found him sitting in the shade of a big old pin oak tree, drinking soda from a can.

Max went and sat beside his friend. "How's your hip?" he asked.

"It hurts," Keith said. "But I'm sure it'll be okay. I think I just need to rest it awhile." He shifted slightly and leaned back against the tree, wincing a little. "Man, I never fell so hard in my life. It didn't hurt this much when I fell off on the thistles!"

"You don't look so good," Max said. He was worried about his friend. Keith's very tan face was pale beneath his longish black hair. Beads of sweat stood out on his forehead. "Should I go get somebody? You want me to find Haley?"

"No way!" Keith warned. Haley was Keith's fourteen-year-old sister. "If you tell Haley, she'll tell my mom, and they'll make me go to the doctor or something. Then I won't be able to ride in the show this weekend. I'll be fine, really," Keith insisted.

"Okay," Max said reluctantly. "You want me to do anything for you?"

Keith shook his head.

Max sat quietly for a moment, considering the gymkhana. Maybe Keith wouldn't think it was such a great idea now that he'd taken a bad fall. "Hey, Keith?" Max spoke up.

"Yeah?"

"What do you think about this gymkhana?" Max tried to sound casual.

"It's about the best way I can think of to make enough money to pay for the Olympic tickets. And it sounds fun! I hope Sharon'll let us do it. In a little bit, when I feel like getting up, we should get Megan and Chloe and go ask her about it."

"Yeah, we should," Max murmured.

"You don't sound like you're into this," Keith observed.

"Oh, I am, I am," Max protested. "I just . . . I never did anything like it before. Don't you think it sounds kind of dangerous?"

Keith frowned. "Dangerous? What do you mean?"

"You know, all those horses running around, with riders waving batons in their faces . . . it just seems like people could fall off a lot, doing that."

"Max, I didn't mean to wave the bat in Popsicle's face. I just got excited. I'm sorry I spooked him," Keith said.

"I know. That's okay," Max said. "I just wish you hadn't fallen off."

"Boy, so do I." Keith rubbed at his side.

"Keith?"

"Yeah?"

Max took a deep breath, then spoke. "Do you ever get afraid when you're riding?"

Keith gave his friend a sidelong glance. "Afraid of what?"

"I don't know, exactly . . ." Max said uncomfortably. "You know, just afraid something will happen. Like an accident, I guess." Max suddenly wished he hadn't brought it up. Now Keith would probably think he was some kind of a scaredy-cat.

"I get nervous sometimes," Keith admitted. "Especially when I'm jumping. And when I go in an English show." Penny went both English and Western. "But I'm not nervous when I'm just riding around here, and never at Western shows. I guess I'm having too much fun to worry about it. Why?"

Max paused, then tried to explain. "I never used to get nervous at all. Like you said, I was always having too much fun to really think about it. But ever since I saw Jump for Joy fall with Amanda, I just can't seem to quit thinking about having an accident like that."

"Max, you know how Amanda rides. She doesn't think. If she'd been paying attention to the other riders and to the slippery footing, Jump for Joy never would've been hurt. You'd never make a mistake like that, right? Hey—" Keith punched his friend playfully in the arm. "Lighten up, dude! We're going to have this gymkhana thing, and it's going to be great!"

Max sighed. "I guess you're right. It could be fun. I just hope everybody doesn't get reckless." He paused. He wanted to tell Keith about the dream he'd been having. Maybe if he talked about it, he'd quit dreaming it. It was really scary. "Keith?" he began. But he was interrupted by a voice from the barn aisle.

"There they are," said the voice. Max and Keith

looked up to see Chloe and Megan approaching. "We've been looking all over for you guys!" Megan said. "Jake's back. Chloe saw his truck come up the drive a little while ago. Let's go find him and ask him about the gymkhana. Then, if he thinks it's a good idea, we'll get him to come with us to ask Sharon."

Max stood up. He held out a hand to Keith, who took it and slowly got to his feet. Careful not to put much weight on his right leg, Keith tested it gingerly.

"Feel better?" Max asked him.

"Some," Keith said. He began walking toward the barn, trying not to limp. "What were you going to ask me, Max?"

Max saw that Keith, Megan, and Chloe were all waiting for him to reply.

"Nothing," Max lied. He pushed the dream out of his mind and followed the others into the barn.

3

THE CHILDREN FOUND JAKE IN THE TRACTOR SHED, working on the harrow attachment he used for raking the rings smooth. As horses traveled around the ring, their feet churned up the footing. If Jake didn't level it out every week, it would become uneven and dangerous. Jake pushed and pulled at a metal piece on the harrow, then stood up and kicked at it with the heel of his worn brown cowboy boots. On the third kick, the piece came unstuck and went sailing through the air. It hit the open door of the shed, missing Max's head by a couple of inches. "Whoa!" Max yelled, jerking back in surprise.

"Max! Gosh, are you okay?" Jake Wyndham hurried over to Max's side. He took Max by the shoulders and looked him over. Jake was tall and lanky, and he had to stoop to look into Max's face. "That didn't hit you, did it?" he asked anxiously, his blue eyes full of concern.

"No," Max said. "It came close, though." There was a good-sized dent in the heavy wooden door near Max's right ear. He bent and picked up the metal piece, which was heavy enough to have knocked him out if it had hit him. His hand trembled a little when he held the part out to Jake.

"Well. It's lucky it missed you." Jake lifted the Atlanta Braves baseball cap he always wore and repositioned it on his head. "I sure didn't see y'all standing there. You must have snuck up on me. Next time, why don't you say something?" Jake took a new part from a paper bag and bent over the harrow. "What do you need?" he asked as he began to fit the part in place.

The four children looked at one another. "Ask him," Chloe whispered to Megan.

"Keith," Megan hissed. "You ask him."

"Jake?" Keith began.

"Hmm," Jake said, busy with the part.

"We had this idea . . ."

Jake stopped pushing the part in place. He squatted on his heels and looked at them suspiciously. "Now, the last time you four had an 'idea,' I ended up chasing loose horses and hunting for missing children all over creation in a thunderstorm in the middle of the night. I hope this idea's better than the last one, or I guarantee I don't want any part of it." He waited for them to speak.

The kids looked at one another again. Jake was talking about the camp-out at the old, supposedly haunted barn. Max remembered how scary it had been when Amanda, and then his sister, had disappeared. Then he remembered all the times he'd *wished* they would disappear!

"Oh, it's nothing like that," Megan said quickly. "We want to have a gymkhana!" She smiled her most winning smile and looked hopefully at Jake.

Max remembered all the times Megan had talked him into being part of her outrageous schemes, against his better judgment. Megan could make almost anything sound like a good idea.

Jake listened while Chloe and Megan explained their plan. Then he bent over his tractor part again. "Well, now, that sounds harmless enough. Chloe, would you pass me that hammer there?"

Chloe handed him the hammer. Max watched Jake's big hand sling the hammer expertly, banging the part into place. He imagined that Jake could fix just about anything. Max wished Jake could fix the uneasy feeling he'd had for the last several days.

"Well, I don't imagine anybody around here has

ever heard of such a thing," Jake went on. "But I reckon we could do it here. You'd have to run it just like a show, send out a prize list and entry forms and all, then see if anybody signs up. But, you know, the one to ask about this is Sharon." Jake took a long bolt from the paper bag and began screwing it into the part. "She's the one who has to okay it."

"We figured we'd have to ask her. But we just wanted to see what you thought about it first," Megan explained.

"I believe she ran into town to pick up some dog food," Jake was talking more to the tractor now than to them. "Why don't you ask her when she gets back?"

"We . . . we were thinking . . ." Megan began.

"We were sort of hoping you'd help us talk to her," Keith said.

"We were hoping you'd ask her for us," Megan admitted. "We know Sharon's so busy with training for the Olympics and all . . . and . . . she likes things done a certain way, you know? She didn't really like it when I asked her about having a Pony Jumper division in the last show. So we thought maybe if *you* told her about the gymkhana first, she might be more likely to listen."

Jake stood up again. He put his hands on his hips and looked down at the children. "So you want me to do your dirty work for you, is that right?"

The four of them nodded their heads hopefully.

"Oh, no," Jake said, bending over the tractor again. "I'm not sure I want to be connected with any more of your schemes. I think you'd better ask her yourselves. Y'all run along now, before I end up knocking one of you in the head with my hammer." Jake herded them out the door and went back to work on the harrow.

"Shoot!" Megan said when they were outside. "I was sure we could get him to ask Sharon for us."

"I guess we have to ask her ourselves." Chloe sighed.

"She'll say yes," Keith said. "Sharon acts really strict sometimes, but inside I think she's a softy."

"That's hard to believe," Megan said doubtfully.

"Did you ever see her talking to Earl?" Keith asked. "She treats him just like a baby." Earl was Sharon's dog, a smart, feisty little Jack Russell terrier. "And you know how she fusses over her horses," Keith went on. "Nah, Sharon just acts tough. Probably because she has to be responsible for this whole barn and all. But she's really nice. At least, she's always been nice to me and my sister."

"Sharon's cool," Max agreed. Maybe this gymkhana would be fun after all, he thought. Jake didn't seem to think it was a bad idea. And if they got lots of people entered, they'd surely make enough money to buy those Olympics tickets. Max began to feel a little better. By the time he got back to Popsicle's stall, he was almost happy again.

He took Popsicle out of his stall and snapped the cross-ties to each side of his halter. Then he began to brush him off, starting from the top of his neck on the left side. Working his way down to Popsicle's front legs and belly, he made sure to brush extra carefully where the girth would touch him. Popsicle's skin was sensitive in that area. If Max didn't get every bit of dirt and dried sweat off him, he'd get girth sores there.

He finished brushing Popsicle's rump and started with his neck on the right side. Max slid his hand over the area he'd cleaned after each brush stroke, feeling for dried sweat and dirt. Popsicle's coppery coat gleamed in the afternoon sunlight slanting through the open door. The horse stood with his eyes drooping shut, enjoying the attention. Max stopped brushing to scratch the special spot on Popsicle's withers, just above his shoulder. The horse groaned with pleasure, leaning into Max's hand. Max smiled and scratched harder.

Keith did a much quicker brush job on Penny and went to get another soda from the machine in the courtyard. "Keith, bring me one?" Max called after him. "I'll pay you back."

A moment later, Keith returned with the soda. After putting Popsicle away, Max sat down on the tack trunk outside his stall. Keith eased himself onto the trunk next to Max. He took a large slurp of root beer, swallowed, and sighed contentedly. Then he burped loudly.

Max laughed. "How do you do that?"

Keith took another swig of soda and burped again. "Like that," he said matter-of-factly.

Max tried it but only let out a feeble-sounding burp.

"Man, that's pitiful!" Keith said. "Try again."

While Max got ready to burp again, Keith watched with an intent expression on his face. Max gulped and let out a tiny burp. Both boys instantly began laughing so hard they nearly fell off the tack trunk.

They were still laughing when the sound of a horse's feet clopped on the concrete floor. The boys looked up to see a big gray horse coming toward them. His head was held high, and his large eyes gleamed as if he were full of mischief. A lead line trailed from his expensive leather halter. The horse's white coat was covered with dirt and grass stains, as if he'd just rolled. He walked by Keith and Max, giving them a nod as if to say hello, then headed for the open door at the end of the barn.

"That's Prince Charming, isn't it?" Keith said.

"Yep," Max said. He eased himself off the trunk. "Guess we should catch him before he jumps the pasture fence. Looks like Amanda let him get loose again."

Max hurried to cut off the big gelding's escape route. He got to the door just ahead of Prince Charming and stood with his arms wide, blocking the opening.

"Whoa, Prince," Max said softly.

Prince stopped and arched his neck, looking at Max as if he were politely waiting for him to move out of his way.

Keith came slowly up on Prince's left side. "Hey, you big dumb white horse," Keith said in a soft, sugary voice. "Come here, you big bonehead."

Prince Charming turned toward the sound of Keith's voice, expecting a carrot. Keith held out his can of soda, which smelled sweet to the horse. Prince Charming curled his upper lip up in a monkey face, trying to find the treat. At that moment, Max stepped forward and picked up the lead line.

Just then, Amanda Sloane came down the aisle, looking for her horse. Unlike most of the other kids, who zipped their chaps on over their shorts in the hot weather, Amanda was always decked out in fancy riding attire. Today she wore pale gray jodhpurs and a lavender riding shirt with a monogram on the little choker collar. There were matching purple ribbons at the ends of her perfect blond braids.

"Prince Charming, there you are," Amanda exclaimed in an exaggerated Southern accent. "Why, I have been searching all over for this horse," she said, without sounding particularly happy to have found him. She looked a lot happier to see Max. She smiled sweetly at him. "How ever did you find him, Max?"

Max shrugged. "He just came walking down the aisle, so we figured we'd better catch him. Here you go." Max held out the lead line to Amanda, who took it hesitantly.

"You are a bad boy, Prince," she scolded, in a voice that was supposed to sound stern. Max thought she actually sounded nervous. Prince Charming was Amanda's new horse. The Sloanes had bought him for her after Jump for Joy was injured. He was a big, silly, thoroughbred–quarter horse cross. Sharon Wyndham had told the Sloanes she thought Prince Charming was too much horse for Amanda to handle, but they had been so impressed with the horse's looks that they ignored her advice.

The horse *was* handsome, Max had to agree. But Prince was more thoroughbred than quarter horse—more stubborn than smart. He was always getting loose somehow and jumping the pasture fence. Unlike most horses, he always ran *away* from the barn whenever he got loose. Once it had taken Jake two whole days to find him and catch him.

Max could tell that Amanda was afraid of her horse. He'd never been afraid of Popsicle, not for a minute. Watching Amanda hold the lead line gingerly and eye her horse nervously, Max almost felt sorry for her.

"How did he get loose this time?" Max asked Amanda.

"He was turned out in the paddock. I went to catch him, and as soon as I put the lead line on him, he just took off trotting. I tried to hang on, but he wouldn't stop, so I just had to let go." Amanda made a little helpless gesture with her hands. "Just look at my jodhpurs," she said, gazing with distaste at the big smear of dirt across her expensive riding pants. "My mother is not going to be pleased."

Max winced at the mention of Amanda's mother, Pamela Sloane. He glanced around to be sure she was nowhere in sight. If Amanda was difficult, Mrs. Sloane was just impossible.

"By the way, Max," Amanda said, "you're still invited to have dinner at our house. Mama said anytime would be fine. How about tonight?" She gave him her best beauty-pageant smile.

For some reason that Max didn't understand, Amanda was annoying and rotten to everybody except him. She was always inviting him to go places with her and asking dumb questions just to start a conversation. Max didn't know why she was always nice to him, but he did know it made him uncomfortable. He usually went out of his way to avoid her, but Amanda always seemed to find him. He suspected that she might even have let Prince Charming loose in the barn just so Max would catch him and she'd have an excuse to talk to him. It was the sort of thing she would do.

"Max?" Amanda said. "What about dinner?"

"I, um . . . gosh, Amanda, I . . . can't," Max stammered. "I'm already expected for dinner at . . . Keith's house. Right, Keith?" Max looked at his friend with a "help me" expression on his face.

"Uh, right," Keith quickly agreed. "Dinner. My house. Right." Keith was barely holding back a laugh.

Max glared at him and gave him a small kick in the shin. "So, I can't go," Max finished. "Hey, Keith, it's getting late. Don't you think we'd better get our stuff together and go wait for your mom?"

"Yeah," Keith said. "I guess so."

"Well, another time, then," Amanda said brightly. "How about tomorrow?"

"Gotta go. 'Bye," Max said, pretending not to

hear her. "Let's get out of here," he growled at Keith, "before she thinks of something else to invite me to."

Max took Keith's elbow and pulled him toward the wash stalls. He peered anxiously around the corner to be sure Amanda was leading Prince Charming back to his stall in the main aisle. As she walked by, she smiled and waved at Max. He backed up, so he could pretend not to see her, and tripped over the raised edge of the wash stall. Stumbling backward, he landed seat first in a big bucket of sudsy water someone had left unemptied after bathing a horse!

Keith began to laugh hysterically. For a few seconds, Max just sat in the bucket, startled and soaking wet. Then he began to laugh, too. He laughed so hard, he didn't even notice Megan and Chloe come into the barn. When they saw Max sitting in the bucket, they both looked surprised.

"What happened to you?" Megan asked her brother.

Max looked up at the sound of his sister's voice and stopped laughing.

"I felt like going for a swim," he said casually. But when he glanced over at Keith, he couldn't keep a straight face. Keith let out a snort, and they started laughing even harder. Megan and Chloe just stood there looking bewildered.

Max tried getting out of the bucket but found it more difficult than he'd thought it would be. Keith tried to pull Max up, but he was really stuck in the bucket, which was even funnier than just falling into it.

"Keith, help!" Max giggled weakly. Finally, with the girls' help, Max managed to get up and on his feet. He stood there, dripping and still laughing.

"I think we should make up a gymkhana game where you have to sit in a bucket," Megan said.

"Oh, yeah, and make the bucket full of something gross, like mud!" Keith said.

"Pudding!" Max offered.

"How about ice?" Chloe said. "That way, nobody's clothes would get too dirty."

"Yeah, ice! Great idea, Chloe," Megan said. She began writing it down in the notebook she carried.

Then they heard a strange noise coming from the direction of the main aisle. There was a scuffling sound, mixed with the scrabbling of a horse's feet on the concrete floor of the barn.

"What was that?" Max said.

They heard someone shouting, and then a bloodcurdling shriek!

4

THE SHRIEKS WERE COMING FROM THE MAIN AISLE, Max, Megan, Keith, and Chloe looked at one another with alarm. Nobody was laughing now.

"Come on!" Max yelled, and he headed for the main aisle with Megan and Chloe on his heels and Keith limping along behind. Max went as fast as he could, without actually running. He knew that a horse could spook at a person running through a barn.

He came around the corner, expecting to see some sort of terrible accident. What he saw made him stop abruptly. Megan bumped into him from behind.

A large wheelbarrow full of horse feed had been

overturned in the middle of the floor. Prince Charming stood over it, eating his way through the pile as fast as he could. Amanda was right beside him, with one hand on his halter, still shrieking at the top of her lungs. Sharon's Jack Russell terrier, Earl, stood near them, barking excitedly.

"Help! Oh, help, please!" Amanda begged.

Max was puzzled. Why was she screaming like that? Why didn't she just pull Prince's head out of the feed, or let go and get a lead line? Prince took a step forward and shoved his nose deep into the mixture of oats and pellets. Amanda shrieked again as he jerked her forward. Then Max realized what the trouble was. Amanda's hand was stuck in Prince Charming's halter!

Max hurried to her side. He could see how Amanda's fingers were wedged under the noseband of the halter, which was a little small for the horse's big head. As long as the horse was eating, his jaws kept the noseband too tight for Amanda to get her hand out. Max needed to get the horse away from the feed, but he didn't want to spook him. The big horse might drag Amanda through the barn or even into the pasture. She could really get hurt.

"Meg! Find a lead line!" Max called.

"What in the world is going on? Who is doing all that screaming?" Allie Tatum, the head groom at Thistle Ridge, come out of the barn office, letting the screen door bang shut behind her. "I go in the office for one minute, and everybody goes crazy around here. I'm trying to place an order on the phone, and I can't even hear myself think!" She came toward them with her hands on her hips. "Now, what have you—?" she started to say. The expression on her face went from stern to alarmed as she saw what had happened.

"Allie, can you hold his head? I can't get this undone . . ." Max motioned to the halter. Every time he tried to unbuckle it, Prince Charming jerked away and Amanda howled.

Allie hurried to his side. "Amanda, hush up!" she said. "We're going to help you." Allie put her strong arms around the big horse's neck in a bear hug. "Unbuckle it now, Max," she instructed.

Max quickly unbuckled the halter. Amanda pulled her hand away, and Max rebuckled the halter so that the horse couldn't escape. Megan came up with the lead line and clipped it on. Allie let go of the horse's head, took the lead line, and, with a couple of mighty tugs, managed to get Prince Charming's head out of the feed.

"Oh, my poor hand," Amanda said, holding her hand close to her chest.

"Amanda Sloane, you know better than to lead a horse by his halter," Allie lectured her. "You're lucky he didn't drag you out the door and into the pasture. It's a good thing Max was there to help you."

"Oh, Max, thank you so much! If it weren't for you, I might have been seriously injured!" Amanda gushed.

Max didn't really like for people to make a fuss when he did something helpful. He'd just done what needed to be done. He started to say it was okay, but before he had a chance to speak, Amanda threw her arms around him and kissed him on the cheek!

Max was stunned. Amanda looked at him adoringly.

Keith and Megan began to laugh. Allie was trying not to, but she couldn't hide the amused look on her face.

Max was horrified. He felt his face instantly turn hot and red with embarrassment. Without a word, Max backed away from Amanda and bolted out of the barn, forgetting the rule about running around horses. He didn't really know where he was going; he just knew he wanted to get as far from the barn as he could—and fast.

"Max, wait," he heard Allie call out.

But he didn't stop. He didn't even turn around. He ended up at the hay barn down near the back pasture fence. The old door creaked as he pushed it open and closed itself with a sigh behind him.

Sweet-smelling bales of hay were stacked nearly to the ceiling. Max quickly climbed as high as he could among the bales.

The air was hot and still in the hay barn. Shafts of sunlight sneaked through the cracks between the rough oak planks that formed the walls. Max sat with his back against the prickly bales of hay and stared fiercely at the dust particles swimming through the beams of light. A wasp buzzed angrily against the tin roof, searching for a way out. Max thought he knew just how that wasp felt.

Max tried to think of some way to undo what had just happened to him, but he was pretty sure that he'd just have to stay in the hay barn forever. How could he go back to the stables and pretend that everything was normal? Amanda had actually *kissed* him. Why did she have to go and do a thing like that? And, worse, she had kissed him right in front of everybody, including his sister and his best friend! Megan would never let him hear the end of it at home. And Keith was bound to tease him about it. Max sighed. Though he was drenched with sweat now from the stifling hot air, he wasn't about to leave the barn. At least, not until he was sure Amanda had gone home for the day.

A strange scrabbling sound came from the floor of the barn, followed by a bark Max recognized as Earl's. In a few moments, the little terrier had scrambled his way up the hay bales. Earl sat down next to Max, then looked at him with his large, patient brown eyes as if he were waiting for Max to tell him all about his troubles.

Max scratched Earl gently behind his ears. "Hey, Earl. You're a good dog."

Earl's stubby tail thumped on the hay bale. He stood on his short legs and licked at Max's face. Max couldn't help smiling. "You can kiss me anytime you want, Earl," Max told him. "But from now on, I'm staying far away from Amanda Sloane." Remembering what Amanda had just done to him, Max shuddered.

The barn door creaked as someone opened it. "Max?"

Max recognized Keith's voice but said nothing. He wasn't sure he felt like talking to anybody right then.

"Max?" Keith said again. "Are you in here?"

Max sighed. "Yes," he answered.

"Where are you?"

"I'm up here." Max leaned over so that Keith could see him from his perch at the top of the stack of hay bales.

Keith clambered up and sat down nearby. For a few moments, the two boys just sat. The corrugated tin roof ticked in the heat. The wasp still beat against it. Max felt too upset to speak. He was ashamed of what had happened before, and angry at Keith for laughing at him. He patted Earl and waited for his friend to say something.

Finally, Keith spoke. "Man, it's hot up here. How can you stand it?"

Max shrugged and looked up at a corner of the roof. He concentrated on staying angry and hoped he wasn't going to cry.

"Hey, Max, I'm sorry I laughed when Amanda, um, you know . . . did that—kissed you."

"I wouldn't have laughed at you," Max said quietly.

"I know. Amanda's such an airhead. I shouldn't have laughed at you. What she did must've been awful," Keith told him.

"You have no idea," Max said quietly.

"Nobody thinks it was your fault," Keith offered. "Everybody just thinks Amanda's a ditz-brain. Prince Charming could have dragged her all over the place. She was lucky that you helped her out."

"I almost wish I hadn't," Max said.

"I can't believe she actually *kissed* you," Keith went on. "That is so *gross.*"

"Tell me about it," Max said. "I guess she *likes* me or something. I wish she'd just be rotten to me like she is to everybody else. Or else I wish she'd just leave me alone." He pulled a handful of hay from the bale underneath him and threw it hard into the air. It fell gently to the floor below. He felt just a little better since Keith had apologized for laughing at him. But something else was still bothering him. "Hey, Keith?"

"Yeah?"

"You won't tell anybody else about this, will you?" Max said anxiously. "You know, if any of the older kids found out about it, they'd never let me live it down." He thought worriedly of Keith's big sister, Haley, who also kept a horse at Thistle Ridge Farm. There was a whole group of teenagers who rode and hung out there. If Haley found out that Amanda had kissed him and told the other kids, it could be a disaster!

"No way," Keith said firmly. "I would never tell *anybody* about it."

"You won't tell Haley?"

"No way. Never," Keith promised.

"Because, you know, a thing like that could ruin my whole riding career here," Max reminded him. "Just imagine if somebody like Tyler Lamar found out. He could torture me for *years* over a thing like this."

"I won't tell anybody," Keith reassured his friend. "But what about Megan and Chloe and Allie? They saw it, too."

"Chloe won't say anything if we ask her not to. And I know enough stuff about Megan that I could bribe her not to tell. Do you think Allie will say anything about it?" Max asked.

Keith shook his head. "Allie's cool."

"Yeah, but she's a girl," Max said warily. "You know how girls are. What if she tells Jake and Sharon?"

"Max, why don't you just try to forget about it?

Maybe you'll feel better if you pretend it never happened," Keith suggested.

"I wish I could forget about it," Max muttered.

"If we don't get out of this hot hay barn, you won't have to worry about it anymore because our brains will be melted. Come on." Keith began to climb down the hay bales.

Max slowly turned around and started to climb down, too. Then he heard a strange little noise. He stopped and tilted his head, trying to hear where the sound had come from.

"Maybe we can go for a swim in the pond," Keith was saying from the barn floor below.

"Shh," Max told him.

"Why? What is it?"

"Listen," Max whispered.

Both boys were silent in the dim barn. The hay crackled as Max shifted his weight. Then he heard the sound again, a soft, high-pitched squeaking, coming from somewhere nearby.

"What is that?" Keith asked, climbed back up the hay bales to join Max.

"I'm not sure . . ." Max looked carefully around him, trying to see what might be making the sound. Then Earl gave a little gruff bark and trotted across the hay. He lay down on his belly before a dark hollow between two bales of hay and sniffed excitedly, his stumpy tail wagging fiercely. Max and Keith crawled across several bales of hay and knelt beside Earl, peering into the hollow between the bales.

The squeaking sound was coming from the hollow. Max tried to see what could be in there, but it was too dark, and he was afraid to reach inside. What if it was a rat?

Suddenly, Max knew what the sound was. "Kittens" he crowed. "There are kittens in there."

"Fancy must've had her babies," Keith said.

Fancy was the little brown-spotted brindle cat who lived at Thistle Ridge. Max had visited plenty of barns, and he knew that barn owners always kept a few cats around to keep the mice and rats from eating all the horse feed. Fancy Dancer, as she was formally known, was queen of all the barn cats at Thistle Ridge Farm.

Max carefully pushed one of the hay bales aside so that he could see. Nestled in the cozy hollow in the hay were four baby kittens. Two were gray tabbies, one was a motley, brindle color like its mama, while the fourth baby was white with gray ears, a gray spot on its head, and a gray tip on its tiny tail.

"Wow, I've never seen such small kittens," Max said softly. "How old do you think they are?"

"Their eyes are still closed, so they must be less than a week old," Keith told him.

"They're so cute," Max said, stroking the brindle kitten's head with one finger. The kitten raised its head and tried to stand on its short, wobbly little legs as it searched for its mama. The other babies began to squirm and cry out. Max could see their teeny, perfect teeth and their little pink tongues. He just had to hold one of them. Smiling, he reached for the little white-and-gray one.

He gently scooped the kitten up and brought it close to his face, amazed at how light it was. The kitten sniffed at Max's lips, tickling him with its whiskers. He held the kitten out a little so he could look at it. It seemed to be all head and belly. Its stubby little legs quivered as it struggled to hold its head up. Max held the kitten close to his face again, enjoying the soft warmth against his cheek. Keith was holding one of the gray tabbies. Earl nosed at the kittens excitedly.

"Careful, Earl," Max told the little dog. "They're just tiny babies. You have to be very gentle."

Max set his kitten gently down in the hay where he'd found it. Then he heard the *meow* of an adult cat. The babies heard, too, and began their odd squeaking again. In another second, Fancy appeared on top of the hay bales, purring loudly.

Then she saw Earl, and her purring changed to a loud, angry hiss.

"Uh-oh," Max said.

5

EARL AND FANCY WERE OLD ENEMIES. MOST OF THE time, cats and dogs who live together get used to each other and learn to get along peacefully. Earl never bothered with any of the other cats. Neither did Merlin, Jake's Border collie. But Fancy was another story. Maybe it was because she was the oldest of all the barn cats and had lived at Thistle Ridge longer than any of the pets. Maybe she thought Earl needed to show more respect for her.

Earl had come to Thistle Ridge two years ago, when he was just a Jack Russell puppy. On his first day there, when he was even smaller than a cat, he'd taken one look at Fancy and gone after her! He still carried a scar from that first encounter—a torn ear from a well-placed swipe from one of Fancy's sharp claws. Jake had to pull the two of them apart.

Now Earl outweighed Fancy by a few pounds, but she could still hold her own in a battle with him. Fancy would see Earl all the way across the barn and come after him hissing, with her ears pinned flat against her head and her tail puffed up to twice its size. And they wouldn't quit fighting until somebody came and separated them. When Fancy and Earl crossed paths, the whole barn knew about it!

"Keith, grab Earl!" Max shouted.

But it was too late. Fancy had seen her enemy. And to make matters worse, he was threatening her babies. The little cat hissed angrily. She growled a deep, loud warning growl that sounded like it ought to have come from a much larger animal. Then she launched herself at the dog.

Earl was ready for her. His brown eyes gleamed as he saw Fancy come at him. He had just enough time to bark at her before she landed on top of him. The two of them rolled and bounced down the hay bales to the barn floor below, making enough noise for an army of cats and dogs.

"Come on!" Max yelled, scrambling down the hay.

Keith quickly replaced the kitten and hurried

down after Max. Max was trying to catch Earl, but the dog and the cat were fighting so furiously, he couldn't get his hands on Earl long enough to pick him up. Fancy and Earl rolled over and over in the dusty hay.

Max spotted a hose coiled near the door. He ran to the spigot, twisted the handle, and, after a splutter or two, water gushed from the hose. Dashing back inside, he aimed the hose at Earl and Fancy, spraying them with cold water.

Fancy gave a howl of annoyance and sprinted up the hay bales, back to her kittens. Earl squinted his eyes and shook his head in what looked like disgust at both getting wet and giving up the fight. Max turned off the hose.

"Wow," was all Keith could say.

"Those two sure do hate each other," Max remarked.

Earl shook himself and trotted out the door. Max made sure the little dog was on his way back to the barn. Then he climbed back up the hay.

"I'm going to put the hay bales back like they were," he explained to Keith. Fancy was busy trying to lick herself dry. Her tiny kittens crept around her, crying loudly for her to lie down with them.

"Those are pretty babies you have there, Fancy," Max told the little cat. Fancy finished licking herself and lay down. The babies cuddled up to her belly and began to eat. Fancy purred contentedly. She seemed to have forgotten all about Earl.

Max carefully moved the hay bales closer together so that Fancy and her kittens were hidden again, safe in the dim hollow between the bales. Then he climbed down and met Keith outside. The two trudged back up the hill to the barn.

Megan and Chloe were waiting for them by Popsicle's stall. "Where have you guys been?" Megan asked impatiently. "Sharon's back from town. Let's go ask her about having the gymkhana."

Max, Keith, and Chloe followed Megan to the barn office. Outside the screen door, they paused. They could hear Sharon inside, talking on the phone. After a few minutes, they heard her hang up. They all looked at one another.

"Well, here goes," Megan whispered. She knocked softly on the wooden frame of the door.

"Come in," Sharon called.

They filed in and stood before the desk where Sharon sat. It was a big rolltop desk that looked like it might have come from an old plantation home. She finished writing something in an appointment book and then turned around to face the children.

Max guessed that Sharon Wyndham was in her early thirties, though she looked younger. She wore her blond hair in a ponytail most of the time, to keep it out of her face. Her bright blue shirt matched her eyes, and she wore tall black riding boots that laced across the foot. Max could tell they were custom-made; he'd gotten a pair of tall boots for his last birthday, but his were off-the-shelf. His mom said she'd get him custom boots when he promised to stop growing.

Sharon always looked neat and clean, no matter how many horses she'd ridden that day or how many stalls she'd mucked out. Her lipstick always looked like she had just put it on. Max never paid too much attention to how people looked, but he thought if he were a grown-up, he might think Sharon was pretty. She was one of the best riders he'd ever seen, and without a doubt the best trainer he'd ever had. Sometimes he still couldn't believe his good luck, that he was actually training with an Olympic rider.

Sharon looked at each of their faces. Nobody spoke. "Yes?" Sharon finally prompted. She crossed one long leg over the other and waited for someone to speak.

"Hey, Sharon." Keith grinned at her.

"Hey, Keith." Sharon nodded.

They were all quiet. Megan was wringing her hands nervously behind her back.

"Is that all you came in here for?" Sharon asked. "To say 'hey'?"

"We . . . um . . .," Megan began.

"We want to ask you something," Chloe said.

"I figured," Sharon observed. "Well, what is it?"

Max spoke up. "You know how we've been trying to earn money to buy tickets to the Olympic games this summer?"

Sharon nodded.

Max went on. "Well, we think we have an idea how we could do it, but we need your permission . . . actually, we need your help."

"We need Thistle Ridge Farm," Megan blurted out.

"We want to sponsor a gymkhana," Chloe explained.

"We think if we put it on, we could raise enough money to buy tickets to the Olympic games," Keith finished.

They all looked at Sharon hopefully, to see what she would say. One eyebrow shot up toward her blond hair. Her blue eyes opened a little wider, and at the same time, her mouth closed a little bit tighter, as if she might be hiding a smile. "A gymkhana?" she finally said.

"Yeah, it's like a horse show but with mounted games instead of equitation classes or jumping classes," Megan said quickly. "There are team games and individual events for all levels of riders. Chloe, show her the book," Megan commanded. Chloe stepped forward and opened the book.

"I know what a gymkhana is," Sharon interrupted.

"Oh," Megan said meekly. "Of course you do. Sorry."

Sharon took Chloe's book anyway and began flipping through it. "Is this where you got the idea?" she asked.

They told her it was.

"I used to compete in gymkhanas when I was a kid," Sharon told them, studying one of the photographs in the book. "They are a great way to develop team spirit and cooperation between horse and rider. And they're just plain fun," she added.

"So could we try to have one?" Megan asked.

Sharon finished looking through the book and handed it back to Chloe. "I'll tell you what," she said. "I don't have a whole lot of time to run a show right now. As you know, the Olympic trials are coming up, and I'm very busy preparing for them. So how about this—you guys do all the planning and preparation for the gymkhana, and I'll let you have it here, at Thistle Ridge. I warn you, though, there's quite a lot of work involved: planning the games, sending out the prize lists, ordering ribbons, processing the entries. Think you can handle it?"

"The Short Stirrup Club can handle anything, can't we, guys?" Megan said enthusiastically.

"Sure we can," Chloe agreed.

Max and Keith nodded.

"Okay, then. Now, there's one more thing. I was just on the phone with a man from another barn in the area. He called me because he's looking for quiet school horses for a handicapped riding program he's setting up. I don't have anything for sale right now that would suit his needs, but how about this? How about if you agree to give a portion of your profits from the gymkhana to the handicapped riding program?"

"Sure," Max said.

"That's cool," Keith agreed.

"What a great idea!" Chloe said.

"Maybe we can help them out, when they get it started," Megan added.

Sharon smiled. "Good. I thought you'd agree. So a third of the profits from the gymkhana can be for your Olympics fund. Another third goes to Thistle Ridge Farm for the use of the facility. The other third you donate to the handicapped riding program. Now, I have one more suggestion. You're going to want local people to come to your gymkhana. It's not like a recognized horse show where people enter to earn points toward year-end awards. So you have to make it worth people's while to come. How about this? I'll put up four tickets to the Olympic games as a prize for the gymkhana team with the most points at the end of the day. You can advertise that on your prize list when you sent it out. How does that sound?"

"Sharon, that's just great!" Megan gushed.

"Awesome!" Chloe agreed.

"Cool!" Keith said.

"I sure hope we win the tickets!" Max said.

"Good luck," Sharon told them. "And you'd better get started." She pulled out a calendar and pointed to a Saturday. "This is the best day to have it. That gives you three weeks to mail out your prize lists and get ready for the event." She got up and went to the old wooden filing cabinet that stood near the desk. She rummaged through one of the drawers and pulled out a small booklet. "Here you go," Sharon said, handing the booklet to Max. "It's a sample prize list to help you plan this thing."

"Thanks, Sharon," Max said. He was starting to feel better about the gymkhana, now that he knew Sharon thought it was a good idea. He tried to imagine her playing mounted games when she was a young girl, but he simply couldn't picture Sharon any other way than she looked now. An image popped into his head: stern, dignified Sharon in red lipstick and the jodhpurs and paddock boots children wore, with her long legs wrapped around a pony. He couldn't help chuckling. Then he noticed Sharon looking at him curiously.

"What's so funny, Max?" she asked.

"Nothing." Max coughed exaggeratedly into his fist. "Just got something in my throat. Must be some dust or something," he explained, thumping his chest with his first.

"Dust?" Sharon raised her eyebrow.

"Thanks a lot, Sharon," Megan said. "We'll get back to you when we have the gymkhana all planned."

"You do that," Sharon said.

Outside the barn office, they all looked one another, their faces full of expectation and excitement. They hurried around the corner to the second aisle, just outside Popsicle and Pixie's stalls. Then they all began talking at once.

"I can't believe she said yes! We can actually have a gymkhana!" Megan said gleefully.

"Sharon is so cool," Chloe said, her voice full of admiration. "Can you believe she's actually going to put up Olympics tickets?"

"She's the best!" Keith said. "I told you she'd say yes."

"Let's see the book, Chloe," Max said.

They all sat down on Max's trunk and began flipping through Chloe's book. "There are so many games in here, I don't know how we'll ever decide which ones to use," Megan said.

"Well, we should probably choose the ones that need the least amount of extra equipment," Max said thoughtfully. "The less stuff we have to deal with, the better."

"Good idea, little brother."

Max made a face at her. His sister was a whole twenty minutes older than he was and never missed an opportunity to remind him of it. Chloe took the book and began reading out loud the descriptions of games that sounded fun and easy to set up. Megan listed the games and the equipment they would need in her notebook.

As he listened to Chloe read the instructions for playing the games, Max had to admit they really did sound like fun. He was already imagining winning the barrel elimination, which involved jumping over a course of oil drums laid end to end. Even the scary dream he'd been having didn't seem like such a big deal anymore.

"Okay, Chloe, read us the list of events," Megan said when they'd finished going through the book.

Chloe read out the games they had chosen. "Flag race, sack race, dress-up race, run-and-ride race, barrel elimination," she read. "We have a lot of races here, don't we?"

"Yes, but they're all different," Keith pointed out.

"They all sound like fun," Max admitted. "Especially the one where you jump over the oil drums. Popsicle will be great at that one."

"Read the rest, Chloe," Megan urged.

Chloe went on. "Obstacle course, Gretna Green—"

"What's that one again?" Keith interrupted.

"It's the one where you ride in and out of the bending poles to your partner, then you ride back holding hands. If you knock over a pole, you're eliminated," Megan reminded him.

"Oh, yeah," Keith said. "Hey, Max, you and I will be great at that one, huh?"

"Yeah, I guess we will," Max said. He was thinking how Penny and Popsicle were so fond of each other. It would be easy to stay close enough together to bend through the poles holding hands with Keith as his partner.

"No fair!" Chloe protested. "Those two horses are crazy about each other. You two are bound to win that one!"

"Chloe, we'll be on your team," Max pointed out.

"Oh. Right." Chloe grinned. "I guess that's good." Then she frowned. "But it's going to be hard to get Bo Peep to go that close to anybody."

Bo Peep was the beautiful, black Exmoor pony that Chloe rode. She belonged to Thistle Ridge Farm, but Sharon let Chloe ride her pretty much whenever she pleased, as long as she wasn't needed in a lesson. Bo Peep had the prettiest face and the fattest neck Max had ever seen. Like most wise old school ponies, when she was good, she was very,

very good, but when she was bad, you had better be able to sit a buck! Max knew Chloe was thinking about how Bo Peep hated to be crowded by other horses when she was in a bad mood.

"Maybe Bo Peep will like the gymkhana games, Chloe," Max suggested.

"I sure hope so," Chloe said.

"We'll have one advantage, Chloe," Megan said.

"What's that?"

"We'll be riding ponies, so it'll be easier for us to mount and dismount," Megan pointed out.

"That's true," Chloe agreed.

"And if we fall off, we'll be a lot closer to the ground!" Megan joked. Everyone laughed.

"Please, let's not talk about falling off," Keith said. "My hip is still sore from when I fell off Penny today."

Max had nearly forgotten about Keith's fall. When he was reminded of it, the uneasy feeling he'd been carrying around returned, and he felt his stomach do a little flip. He tried to think about something else.

"So we're a team for this thing, right, guys?" Megan was saying. "The Short Stirrup Club is going to win the gymkhana. Then we can go to the Olympics!"

"Right," Keith said. "Come on, put your hands in." He stuck his hand out, palm down. Megan placed her hand on top of his. Chloe laid a hand on top of Megan's.

"Max!"

Megan's voice startled Max. He realized they were all waiting for him to join them, so he stuck his hand on top of the others and said with them, "Short Stirrup Club!" just the way they always did before a horse show or anytime they got together to help each other out. But Max's heart wasn't in it. He noticed Megan looking at him curiously, so he avoided her gaze. He wasn't sure himself why he was dreading this gymkhana. He just wished the terrible feeling would go away.

They spent the rest of the afternoon drawing up the prize list. Then they gave it to Sharon to have printed up and mailed out.

"Well, that's all done," Megan said, sounding satisfied. "Now all we have to do is wait for the entry money to roll in."

"That's not all we have to do," Chloe reminded her. "We also have to get the equipment together, and get someone to judge, and call the food truck to come out." Chloe was pointing to items on a list she'd been carrying around. "We also have to get an announcer, and have the emergency medical team standing by, and section off the ring—"

"And we have to practice! If we want to win those

Olympics tickets, our team has to be prepared," Megan said.

"Who do you think the other teams from Thistle Ridge will be?" Chloe asked.

"My sister Haley will want to be in the gymkhana," Keith said. "And she'll probably get Tyler Lamar to be on her team. And Melissa and Scott."

"Do you think Haley and Tyler like each other?" Megan asked "They sure do spend a lot of time together."

"Who cares?" Keith shrugged. "Tyler's so annoying. And Haley's always telling me what to do with Penny, like I don't know anything about horses. They can have each other."

"You want to know something?" Chloe lowered her voice. The other kids leaned toward her, eager to hear some sort of sensational news. "Last week, when I went to the back paddock to bring Bo Peep up from turnout, guess what?"

"What?" three voices said at once.

"I went by the tree that was struck by lightning, and you know what?"

"What?" Keith repeated.

"I saw Haley and Tyler Lamar, and you know what?"

"What, Chloe?' Megan said impatiently.

"They were *holding hands,"* Chloe said dramatically.

"Gross," Max said.

"No way!" Megan said. "And you waited this long to tell me?"

"I forgot about it until just now," Chloe said.

"Excellent!" Keith said. "I *love* to get dirt on Haley. I can torture her for weeks with this one!"

"Hey, Max, maybe you and Amanda Sloane should be on a team with Haley and Tyler," Megan teased.

"Shut up, Megan," Max snapped.

"Then, after the show, you could go on a double date!" Megan went on.

Max stood up. His stomach still felt squeamish. He wasn't sure he'd ever been so angry at his sister. "I said be quiet," Max said in a low voice.

Keith and Chloe watched uneasily. Neither said a word.

Megan laughed, "Oh, come on, Max. I'm only teasing. Don't be so sensitive."

"Just don't say another word about me and Amanda," Max growled.

"Okay, okay,' Megan said. "Sorry." Then she couldn't help adding, "But if Tyler needs any advice about how to kiss a girl, we'll send him to you."

Max was standing by Megan, who was sitting on his tack trunk. Without a word, he gave her a shove, landing her on her butt on the barn floor. Then he turned and stalked out of the barn, leaving Keith, Chloe, and a very surprised Megan to wonder what was the matter with him.

6

MAX WAS CANTERING POPSICLE DOWN ONE LONG SIDE of the big outdoor ring, which at that moment seemed to go on forever. He was supposed to jump a big stone wall at the far end of the ring, but Popsicle's canter never brought him any closer to the jump. Sharon stood in the middle of the ring. She was calling out some instructions to him, but a wind came up and snatched the words from her lips. Try as he might, Max couldn't understand what she was saying to him.

He cantered on. The sky had been clear and blue a moment before but grew dim and gray as he finally approached the jump. Clouds came from beyond the barn and blew across the sky, vanishing as quickly as they had formed. Max was worried. He knew he was supposed to jump the wall, but it was getting bigger. And there was something underneath it; he couldn't see it, but he knew it was there.

Popsicle tossed his head uneasily. Max looked around, hoping he could see another approach to the fence, but now he saw that there was mud all around him, worse than the mud that Jump for Joy had slipped in. Max had no choice but to canter on toward the jump.

The closer he came to the stone wall, the larger it grew. *How are we ever going to clear that?* he thought frantically. He wanted to pull up, but it was too late. If he stopped now, he might break Popsicle's leg. If he jumped the wall, something worse might happen. He felt terribly afraid and confused. He looked once more to Sharon for advice, but she was busy riding Quasar.

Then he was at the fence. It was time to jump. He bent forward into two-point position and felt Popsicle rock back on his hind legs. Could he clear it?

Popsicle tried to jump the wall. They went up, up, nearly to the top, then, horribly, they began to fall. Max looked down and saw the mud below. Popsicle would surely break a leg. Max had made a terrible mistake! He shouldn't have tried to jump that fence; he should have known it was just too high. He closed his legs around Popsicle's sides, trying to urge the horse upward again, but it was no use. The clouds whirled overhead as he and the horse fell and fell toward the ground.

"Nooooo!" Max cried out. He had been squeezing his eyes shut. When he opened them, he was in his own bed, in his own dark bedroom. He was breathing hard and fast, clutching the quilt that covered his bed as if he were holding Popsicle's reins. He slowly let go of the quilt and wiped at his sweaty forehead.

It was the dream again, the one he'd been having for weeks now, ever since he'd seen Jump for Joy injured. He lay in bed and listened to his heart pounding with fear. He was tired, but he was afraid to close his eyes again. The dream was still too close.

Max got out of bed and started down the hall to his parents' room. But outside their door, he hesitated, suddenly unable to wake them up. With a little rush of sadness, he realized he felt too old to run to his parents when he had a bad dream. He stood in the dark hallway feeling scared and alone.

For a moment, Max considered waking his sister. Maybe if he told her about the dream, he'd feel better. But he was still mad at Megan for teasing him about Amanda. Reluctantly, Max went back to his own room and got under the covers. Afraid to go to sleep, he lay awake for a long time, thinking.

What if the older kids found out that Amanda had kissed him? If they did, he knew they could make his life completely miserable for a long time. He wished he could just forget about it somehow and that everyone else would, too. He squirmed uncomfortably and pushed the thought away.

Then the other thought came back, the one that had been haunting him for weeks. There was a riding camp at Thistle Ridge every summer. One day, the campers had gone on a trail ride and then taken the horses swimming in the lake. For some reason, everyone had fallen off on that trail ride. First Amanda had fallen off Prince Charming. Then Megan fell off when Pixie cantered toward the lake and stopped suddenly. Bo Peep had decided to have a good shake after their swim and had shaken Chloe right off in the process. Then Keith fell off Penny, because the cinch on his saddle was too loose, of course. The only one who didn't fall off that day had been Max.

Max thought back to his very first riding lesson. On his fifth birthday, Max's father had taken him to the stable. Max had ridden an old, woolly Appaloosa named Toby, whose spots had nearly faded with age. He remembered how hard it had been just to keep his heels down; he'd been wearing floppy rain boots that kept slipping out of the stirrups. But mostly he remembered how excited and proud he'd been to finally be up on a horse. And how as soon as he was put in the saddle, he knew he belonged there.

Max could remember lots of things about riding and showing since that first lesson. He could remember the first time he jumped, his first horse show with Popsicle, his first championship ribbon. But there was one thing Max could not remember, and it was bothering him more than anything.

Try as he might, Max could not remember falling off a horse! He'd come close a couple of times, he knew, but somehow he'd always managed to scramble back in the saddle. He'd seen his sister fall off countless times and had gotten so used to seeing Keith fall off that he just expected it now.

But yesterday had been different. Keith had been hurt enough that he didn't get back on. And seeing Megan get run away with as she had the first day they'd ridden into the pastures at Thistle Ridge had really shaken him. He'd been sure his sister would fall off and be trampled, even though she'd actually stayed on all the way back to the barn. And then seeing Jump for Joy slip in the mud and come up on three legs had made him think: What if something like that happened to Popsicle? And what if he, himself, fell and was injured, too?

Max knew everyone fell off sooner or later. He knew he would, too. But he was dreading it so much that it was interfering with his riding. He wished more than anything that he had fallen off when he was younger. Then he'd have it over with, and he'd know what to expect. Max closed his eyes and tried not to think about all the ways someone could fall from a horse.

When he opened his eyes again, it was very early in the morning. Max went downstairs and fixed himself a bowl of cereal. While he ate, he tried to think of a way to stop feeling so worried about falling off his horse. He finished his cereal and pushed the bowl aside. Then he folded his arms and rested his chin on them.

Max wondered if Sharon ever worried about falling off. He remembered seeing her fall off at a big horse show on national television. Could he talk to her about it? Max admired Sharon so much. She always seemed so busy and unapproachable, but he had to admit, every time he had gotten up the courage to go to her about something, she'd always been friendly and willing to listen. He glanced at the kitchen clock. It wasn't even seven o'clock yet. Sharon would be at the barn already, he knew, helping Allie feed and hay and water the horses.

Max decided he might feel better if he could talk to Sharon. He rinsed out his cereal bowl and set it in the sink. Then, taking a piece of paper from a notepad, he wrote on it, "Mom and Dad—I rode my bike to the barn. See you later, love Max."

Max got dressed quickly and quietly slipped out the door. He backed his bicycle out of the garage, strapped on his helmet, and pedaled off down the driveway. Thistle Ridge Farm was a little less than three miles from his house. Max enjoyed riding his bike there.

The sun was just coming up. Max liked the early-morning light and the silvery dew-drenched grass. He liked the quiet when most people were still asleep. Being up that early was like having the world all to himself for a little while.

Soon he was pedaling along the white-fenced pastures in front of Thistle Ridge Farm. In no time, he spotted the familiar green sign with the golden horse jumping over the thistle that marked the entrance to the farm. He pedaled up the long gravel driveway shaded on either side by stately pecan trees. For a moment, he stopped near the closest paddock to the barn to watch the four baby foals that were turned out there to play.

They were the same four babies he'd seen on his first day at Thistle Ridge: two chestnuts colts, a bay mare, and a brown-and-white paint colt that was Max's favorite. The colt's name was Shiloh, after a Native American tribe that had once lived nearby.

Max walked his bike the rest of the way up the hill and left it near an old section of fence nearly hidden by honeysuckle and climbing roses. Then he went into the barn.

Inside the door, Max paused, waiting for his eyes to adjust to the dimmer light. Allie was feeding the horses. The air was full of the sound of them busily munching their grain. Somewhere he heard a horse pawing impatiently at his stall and Allie's sharp "Hey! Be still, there!" Then came the familiar *shoosh* of the feed scoop sluicing through the grain and the musical *thrum* of it hitting the plastic manger in each horse's stall.

Max wanted to go and see Popsicle right away, but first he decided to look in on Quasar. Max stood watching the big warmblood finish his breakfast, admiring his straight, muscular legs and grand, arching neck. Quasar turned his big head sideways in the manger, trying to get at the last few crumbs of his grain. When he was sure there was no more, he sighed, took his head out of the manger, and looked around.

"Hey, Quaze," Max said. Quasar gazed steadily

at Max. He was a calm, happy horse, who knew his job well and loved to do it. Max put a hand up to the bars of the stall. Quasar pressed his face closer to the bars, so Max tried scratching him gently over his eyes. The horse lowered his head, enjoying the attention. Max traced a finger down Quasar's jagged, "broken" blaze to the tip of his nose. Max thought he'd like to draw Quasar. Maybe he'd bring his paper and drawing pencils next time.

"You found his favorite spot."

Max glanced over his shoulder and saw Sharon standing behind him. Her blond hair was tucked neatly into a very old velvet hunt cap. She wore a bright red polo shirt and held a long dressage whip in one hand. Earl stood at her feet, wagging his stumpy tail and panting.

"You're here mighty early this morning," she observed, smiling.

Max gave Quasar one last rub and shoved his hands into the pockets of his cutoffs. "Yeah, I know. I just woke up extra early today, and I couldn't go back to sleep, so I thought I'd come on over here. It's okay, right?" he asked, suddenly anxious that maybe he shouldn't have come so early.

"You know you're always welcome here, Max," Sharon told him. She undid the latch on Quasar's stall and slid the door open. Earl started to follow her inside. "Earl, no," Sharon commanded. "Max, would you grab Earl for me? Thanks," she said when Max had the little dog by the collar.

"Quasar's not too fond of dogs. And Earl's not too bright about horses," Sharon explained as she buckled a leather halter around Quasar's head and led him out of his stall. "It is just beyond me why Jack Russell terriers are considered good horse dogs. I never knew one that didn't somehow get under a horse's feet and get himself kicked." Sharon was shaking her head as she clipped the cross-ties to each side of Quasar's halter. "Oh, you can let him go now, Max. Earl doesn't usually bother horses when they're in the aisle."

Max let go of Earl's collar. The terrier trotted off down the aisle, passing right between Quasar's legs as if he didn't know the big horse was there. Quasar stomped one of his huge feet in annoyance.

"Earl!" Sharon exclaimed. Earl never even turned around. He was off on some doggy errand. "You see?" Sharon said in exasperation. "That dog's got no respect."

"He's cute, though." Max grinned.

"It's true," Sharon agreed. "You have to love him."

Max nodded and looked up at the rafters above. He was trying to work up the nerve to talk to

Sharon about his falling-off anxiety. He took a deep breath and began. "Um . . . Sharon?"

"Yes?"

"Did you know Fancy has kittens hidden in the hay barn?" was what Max said. *Chicken!* was what he thought to himself.

"Is that where she's got them?" Sharon said. "I wondered." She picked up one of Quasar's feet and began to rake the dirt out of it with a hoof pick. "How many has she got?" Sharon moved to the hind foot on the same side and went to work on it.

"Four," Max said. "Two gray tabbies, a brindle that looks just like her, and a white one with gray spots."

"Phew!" Sharon made a face. "Max, hand me that bottle of coppertox, will you?" Sharon picked carefully at a little crack in the bottom of Quasar's hoof.

Max brought her the coppertox and watched with interest as she squirted the bright green liquid on a little piece of a cotton ball and packed it into the crevice. He knew that coppertox was for treating thrush, which is an infection that horses sometimes can get from standing around in a mucky stall. Thrush has a very strong, stinky smell that Max thought was even worse than rotten eggs.

"This horse had a terrible case of thrush when I first got him," Sharon explained as she carefully picked out his other feet and checked them for signs of thrush. "It took weeks to get rid of it. Now his feet are in good shape, except that one hind foot that just seems prone to it." She capped the bottle of coppertox and set it aside. Then she picked up a rubber curry comb and began rubbing Quasar's neck in a circular motion.

Max was only half-listening to her as he watched her pick up a stiff brush and go to work removing the loose dirt the curry comb had lifted from Quasar's coat. This was probably the only chance he'd have to talk to Sharon alone. Soon the barn would be busy and full of boarders and grooms and students. He tried to think how to begin. "Sharon?" he finally asked.

"Yes?"

"I . . . I wanted to talk to you about something . . ." Max scuffed at the barn floor with the heel of one worn paddock boot. He took his hands out of his pockets but didn't know what to do with them. So he shoved them into his pockets again.

"What is it?" Sharon was going over Quasar with a soft brush now, expertly flicking the last bits of dust from his gleaming coat.

Max took a deep breath. *It's now or never,* he thought. He opened his mouth to tell her about his fear of falling, but just as he was about to speak, he heard someone come in. It was Megan.

"Hey, Sharon. Hey, Max," she called out. "Max I

saw your note, so I decided to ride my bike here, too. Boy, is it getting hot out there. I'm already ready for a soda."

Max closed his eyes in frustration and squeezed his hands into fists. Now he couldn't talk to Sharon. Who knew when he'd catch her when she was alone and not too busy again?

"Good morning, Miss Megan," Sharon said, nodding.

"I see you're going to ride Quasar," Megan chirped. "Hey, Max, we need to finish planning his gymkhana. Want to come and help me make a list of all the equipment we'll need?"

"Yeah, sure," Max said gloomily.

"Max, what was it you wanted to tell me?" Sharon straightened up.

"Oh." Max sighed heavily. "Nothing, really. It can wait." He gave Quasar a good-bye pat on the neck, then turned and headed toward the second aisle with Megan right behind him.

7

"... So I FIGURE WE CAN MAKE MOST OF THE EQUIPment we'll need ourselves." Megan was chattering a mile a minute about the gymkhana as Max followed her around the corner to Pixie and Popsicle's stalls. But he wasn't really listening to his sister. He was kicking himself for not talking to Sharon while he'd had the chance. He and Megan were supposed to have a lesson with Sharon later that week. Maybe he'd get another chance to speak to her then.

Max waited for Popsicle to finish his breakfast. Then he went to work grooming him so he'd be all ready to tack up. He had just slipped off Popsicle's green nylon halter and was closing the door of his stall when Keith came in. Max had been feeling pretty alone. He was glad to see his friend.

"Hi!" Max said, expecting to hear Keith's usual friendly "Hey, Max."

But Keith barely mumbled a hello to Max as he walked by. He went straight to Penny's stall without even looking at Max.

Max thought that was pretty strange. *Something must be bothering Keith,* he thought to himself. He went over to Penny's stall and stood in the doorway. "Are you okay?" he asked his friend.

"Sure. I'm fine. Why?" Keith looked up and offered his usual impish grin, but Max still thought that something was not quite right.

"You want to go see the kittens?" Max suggested.

"Yeah, sure. You go on ahead. I just want to groom Penny, and I'll meet you down there," Keith said.

"I'll wait for you," Max offered.

"What kittens?" Megan came over to stand by Max.

"Hey, Megan," Keith said.

"Hi, Keith. What kittens?" Megan repeated.

"Fancy has kittens," Max told her.

"Oh, really? Oh, why didn't you tell me? Let's go see them," she begged. "Where are they? Oh, I wish Chloe would hurry up and get here."

"I'm here," said a husky, sweet voice. Chloe stood

right behind them, with the gymkhana book tucked under one arm, eating a banana.

"Chloe! Max says Fancy has kittens!" Megan said excitedly.

Chloe's green eyes grew wide. "Really?" she said around a mouthful of banana. "Where are they?"

"Yeah, where are they, Max?" Megan pleaded.

Suddenly, Max had an idea. "I'll tell you where they are," Max said, "but you've got to promise something."

"What?" Megan said.

"You have to promise not to tell *anybody* about Amanda kissing me yesterday," Max said. "And don't tease me about it anymore, either." He looked hard at his sister. "Promise?"

Megan shrugged. "Okay," she said. "I promise. Now, where are they?"

"Chloe?" Max looked at her.

"I won't say anything," Chloe said sincerely. "I wouldn't want anybody thinking I let Amanda Sloane kiss *me,*" she added.

"Okay, come on, I'll show you where they are." Max started out the door. He wanted to see them again himself. Especially the little white one with spots.

"How come you didn't make Keith promise not to say anything?" Megan complained.

"Because I know I can trust him. Guys stick together, right, Keith?" Max smiled at Keith. But Keith was looking the other way.

Max led them to the hay barn, where they climbed up the bales and found the kittens curled up with Fancy. They each held one, exclaiming over how cute and tiny they were. Max picked up his favorite spotted kitten and rubbed his nose in the kitten's soft fur.

Suddenly, the dim light in the hay barn brought back the memory of Max's bad dream. Max had to get outside. He shuddered and put the kitten back down with Fancy. He scrambled down the hay and shoved open the barn door, grateful for the bright, hot sunlight outside and the cool breeze that always swept across the ridge.

Sharon was riding Quasar in the dressage ring and Max decided to walk down and watch her. He stood by the fence and rested his elbows on the top rail. Quasar looked magnificent. His coat shone like a new penny in the sunshine and his white stockings flashed as he pranced around the ring. Max couldn't help feeling lifted by the sight of such a beautiful animal. Sharon sat on the horse's big strides like she was a part of him. Max tried to imagine what riding Quasar would feel like. Maybe when he was older, Sharon would let him sit on Quasar.

Sharon made one last pass across the ring. Quasar seemed to be skipping as he did perfect *tempe* changes, switching leads every other stride in the most collected canter imaginable. Watching them, Max realized for the first time that the gaits of the horse really had nothing to do with how fast you were going. It was all about rhythm.

Sharon let Quasar walk, giving him a long rein as a reward. She patted her horse affectionately. Then she saw Max. She must have known how Max admired the big horse, because right then she said something amazing.

"Hey, Max, would you like to walk Quasar out for me?" Sharon asked him.

Max's mouth dropped open. He couldn't believe what he had just heard. Had Sharon Wyndham actually just asked him if he wanted to ride Quasar? Quasar the dressage horse, Quasar the Olympic horse? Max closed his mouth. He swallowed and managed to nod yes.

"Well, then," Sharon said, "go get your helmet."

Max turned and raced up the hill. He remembered to slow down to a very fast walk once he was inside the barn. He yanked his chaps out of his trunk and zipped them over his shorts as fast as he could, remembering to tuck his shirt in. Sharon liked everyone to look neat when they were riding, no matter what. He stuffed his helmet on and fastened the clear plastic harness under his chin, fumbling with the snap because he was so excited. Then he hurried back down to the dressage ring, trying to look casual.

When Sharon saw him coming, she dismounted and began shortening the stirrups for him. Max climbed over the fence and walked to Quasar's left side. The big horse turned his head to see who was approaching. He gazed calmly at Max, ears politely forward, then looked ahead again, waiting patiently for him to mount up.

"Ready?" Sharon asked him.

Max nodded and stepped closer to Quasar, preparing for Sharon to give him a leg up. He took the reins in his left hand and put his right hand toward the front of the saddle, near the pommel. Bending his left knee, he looked up at the saddle, which seemed incredibly far above his head.

"Ready?" Sharon asked, putting her hands around his left leg where he held it up. Max was as ready as he would ever be. "On three," she said to him.

"One, two, three," he counted out loud. On three, he jumped up and felt Sharon give him a boost. Then he was in the saddle. He gathered the reins in his hands as Sharon adjusted the stirrups for him. The reins felt heavy and strange, and the saddle seemed to push his legs into a different position. It had been a while since he had ridden any horse other than Popsicle. He was used to his own saddle and the familiar feel of his own horse's sides under his legs.

Quasar felt immense! Max glanced at the ground. He seemed very far away from it. In fact, he felt much closer to the sky!

"Okay, you're all set." Sharon stuck Max's foot into the off stirrup and gave his leg a pat. "Just walk him around for about ten minutes. He's a big marshmallow." Sharon winked at Max and gave Quasar an affectionate pat. She glanced at her watch. "I have to make a quick phone call, but I'll come check on you in a minute, okay?"

Max nodded, trying to hold back the huge smile that was just about ready to come out. Was this actually happening? He checked to see that there was really a big warmblood horse under him. There was. Max carefully shortened the reins a little, making sure they weren't twisted between the bit and the buckle. Then he tentatively pressed his legs into Quasar's sides, wondering if Olympic dressage horses understood commands the same as chestnut quarter-horses.

To his relief and delight, he felt Quasar obediently walk on. Even at the walk, the horse's stride felt huge. Max guided him gently toward the rail with his left leg and right rein and felt the big horse step willingly across the track. Then he was walking along the rail, letting Quasar cool down after his workout.

"Hey!" Max heard a shout. He looked up and saw Keith waving excitedly at him from the door of the hay barn. In a moment, he saw Chloe and Megan join him. Max thought about waving back at them, but he didn't want to put the reins into one hand. It seemed important to keep holding them properly. Max felt like waving at your friends just wasn't the thing to do while riding an Olympic dressage horse.

He watched them out of the corner of his eye as he continued to walk Quasar around the ring. Megan, Keith, and Chloe ran to stand at the rail, talking excitedly and pointing at him.

"Is it Quasar?" he heard Megan ask.

"It *is* Quasar," he heard Chloe say. "Wow!"

Max felt very important. He knew he'd been given a special privilege. He smiled graciously at them as he passed by.

"Lucky," he heard Keith say.

The next time Max passed by them, he noticed that some more kids were coming down the hill from the barn. They must have seen him riding too. Max recognized Keith's sister, Haley, with her short black hair and very tan skin. Tyler Lamar was right behind her, with a few of the other older kids who rode at Thistle Ridge. They were all coming to see him riding Quasar. Max lifted his chin and walked on, feeling grand. Quasar ambled along underneath him.

He saw Haley whisper something to Tyler. She had one tiny long braid wrapped with brightly colored thread. She twisted it around her finger as she laughed about whatever she had said to Tyler. "Go get her," he thought he heard Tyler say. Haley headed up the hill toward the barn. In a minute, she came back down with Amanda Sloane.

Suddenly, Max began to feel uneasy. The whole time he'd been up on Quasar, he'd felt so happy. The uncomfortable feeling that had been hanging over him for so long had vanished. But now it was back, a hundred times stronger than it had been. Quasar must have felt Max tense up, because he suddenly lifted his head and walked a little quicker.

Though he was trying his best to concentrate on riding Quasar, Max couldn't help noticing that the big kids had bunched together. Then he saw them turn to face him. Something was up; he was sure.

"Ready?" he heard Tyler say.

Then all the big kids, led by Tyler, began to chant loudly, "Max and Amanda sitting in a tree, K-I-S-S-I-N-G!"

Max felt his cheeks turn bright red. His ears felt like they were on fire. He wanted to run away, but he couldn't. Sharon had trusted him to walk out Quasar. He looked toward the barn, hoping to see her, but she was nowhere in sight. All he could do was continue riding as they shouted out the chant a second time.

"Hey, Max, when's the wedding?" Tyler called out. "I hope we're all invited!"

Max wanted to ignore Tyler, but it was impossible. All the big kids were laughing. He looked imploringly at Megan and Keith and Chloe. Megan was saying something to Tyler. Keith had disappeared. Max didn't dare look at Amanda.

Then, to his relief, he saw Sharon in the side doorway of the barn. She started to walk down the hill when she saw everybody standing by the ring. Earl was trotting along ahead of her. Now the kids would forget about teasing him.

Out of the corner of his eye, Max saw Fancy leap up on the fence rail. Max forgot about his own problems when he realized that Earl had also seen the cat. The little dog froze for one second, then took off at a dead run, heading straight for Fancy.

Then Fancy saw Earl. She jumped off the fence, ears flattened, tail fluffed, and ran toward the dog. With dread, Max saw what was about to happen. Fancy and Earl were going to collide—right underneath Quasar!

Max knew that Quasar didn't like dogs. How was she going to react to one fighting with a cat under his feet? Max felt panicked. He couldn't think what to do. He looked at Sharon, who began to run down the hill. She was shouting something at him, but he couldn't hear her over the barking and hissing. Max hoped she would get to him and Quasar before it was too late.

Then, with a yowl from Fancy and a growl from Earl, the cat and dog attacked each other. Quasar snorted, kicked out and jumped straight up in the air! Max lurched forward and landed on Quasar's neck. The horse scooted away from the animals and stood with his nostrils flaring, looking around as if he expected more cats and dogs to come at him from all sides. Max was hanging by his arms around Quasar's neck. He couldn't get back in the saddle, and he couldn't get down, because one foot was stuck in the stirrup. And he was slipping! If he fell off, Quasar might spook, and Max would be dragged by his caught foot. He was really frightened.

Suddenly, Max felt hands around his waist and realized someone was helping him back into the saddle. Max was relieved to feel the comfortable leather under his seat again. He looked to see who had helped him so he could thank the person. It was Tyler! Max couldn't say a word. He picked up the reins and looked away, completely mortified.

Then Sharon was there, making sure he was okay. He heard her tell him not to worry, that she was sorry Earl had run underneath Quasar like that, and that Max had done a good job to stick on. But Max barely heard her. All he could think about was how awful he felt. The big kids had found out about Amanda kissing him, just as he'd feared. And he'd nearly fallen off Quasar, right in front of everybody. Then he'd had to accept help from Tyler, of all people!

Max couldn't wait to dismount. He was numb. He must have handed Sharon the reins. He must have thanked her for letting him get on Quasar. He must have walked by all the kids, but he didn't remember any of it. All Max wanted was to be alone. He had never been so ashamed and embarrassed in all his life.

The first building that crossed his path was the tractor shed. Max stumbled inside. He climbed up on the tractor and sat in the driver's seat. He put his hands on the big steering wheel and stared at it for a minute. Then he put his head down and let the tears come.

Max didn't know how long he'd been in the tractor shed when he finally stopped crying. For a long time, he sat bent over the steering wheel with his head resting on his arms, thinking. A few months ago, moving to a new town was the worst thing that had ever happened to him. Now he wished he could move again. He didn't know how he could ever face all those kids again. He sighed.

"Max?" someone said quietly.

Max was startled. He hadn't known that anyone was in the tractor shed when he came in. "Who's there?" he said suspiciously.

"It's me, Keith."

Keith's voice sounded oddly muffled. Max couldn't see him anywhere. "Where are you?" he asked, looking around.

"Up here."

Max looked up and saw Keith sitting in a canoe that had been stored above him, resting upon the boards that supported each rafter. "How'd you get up there?" Max asked.

Keith pointed to a ladder in the corner. Max understood that he had climbed the ladder and then crawled across the supports to get to the canoe. He thought about joining Keith in the canoe, but it didn't seem worth the effort. He laid his head back down on the steering wheel and closed his eyes.

"Max, are you mad at me?" Keith wanted to know.

"Why should I be mad at you?" Max asked.

"For telling Haley," Keith said sheepishly.

Max froze. "Telling Haley what?"

Keith was silent for a moment. Then he confessed. "For telling Haley about Amanda kissing you."

Max lifted his head and looked at Keith. "You *told?"* Max was incredulous.

Keith nodded.

"How could you tell? You knew she'd tell everybody! Keith! How could you?" Max said in disbelief.

"I'm sorry, Max. She tricked me! She talked like she already knew about it, and I told her without meaning to. I'm really sorry," Keith said. He was nearly crying himself.

Max couldn't believe what he was hearing. As if everything weren't bad enough, now his best friend had betrayed him. If it weren't for those Olympics tickets, he would have quit the gymkhana right then. He climbed off the tractor and stalked out of the barn, not even bothering to close the door behind him.

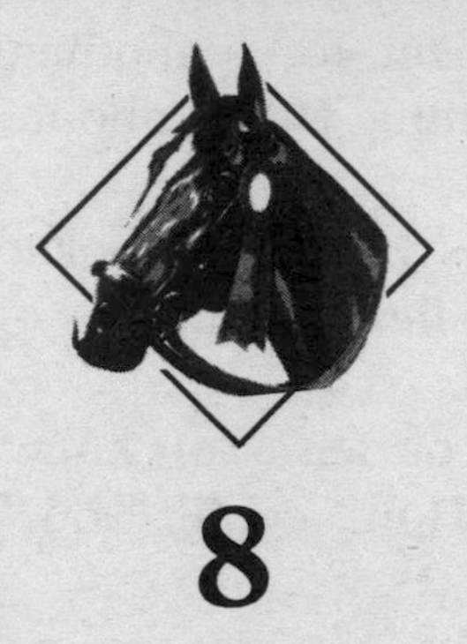

8

THE SHORT STIRRUP CLUB HAD WEEKS LEFT TO PREpare for the gymkhana. The rest of the first week, Max helped Megan, Chloe and Keith round up the equipment for the events, but he was cool toward Keith. Max was having a hard time forgiving Keith and didn't really feel like talking to him.

One day, they found a pile of burlap sacks in the old barn in the back pasture to use for the sack race. Another day, they made flags for the flag race by stapling red vinyl triangles to wooden dowels. Jake gave them some poles that wouldn't splinter to use for bending poles. They also devised an ingenious obstacle course for the last event of the day, which involved lots of tricky maneuvers and even a few jumps. With Jake's help, they measured off the big outdoor ring into lanes for racing, using pieces of string to get the lines even.

The entries had started to come in. Every day there were more. Megan insisted that their team practice whenever the four of them could get together. They all worked on the skills they would need to do well in the gymkhana.

A week before the gymkhana, the four friends were in the outdoor ring practicing handing off batons for the relay race, when Amanda Sloane came mincing down the hill toward them. She had on a bright pink polo shirt with a matching pink bow in her ponytail. Max saw her climb daintily up on the fence and perch on the top rail. She held the rail with her fingertips, as if she were afraid of getting her hands dirty, and watched them practice the handoffs.

"Max," she called to him.

Max pretended he hadn't heard her.

"Max," she called out loudly.

Max pretended to be absorbed with holding a baton.

"MAX!" Amanda yelled.

Max cringed. The whole farm could have heard her yelling his name. He had just about lived down all the teasing he'd taken for Amanda kissing him, and he didn't want everyone to be reminded of it again. Gritting his teeth, he turned and trotted toward her.

"What?" he whispered loudly, hoping none of the big kids were around to see him talking to her.

"What are y'all doing?" she drawled.

"Practicing for the gymkhana," Max told her.

"Now, I have been hearing about this gymkhana," Amanda said. "I am so interested to know what it is."

"It's, you know, games," Max said, sounding annoyed. He was sure Amanda must know what the gymkhana was. Everyone was talking about it. The prize list was even posted on the big bulletin board outside the barn office.

"Well, what kind of games?" Amanda persisted.

"Gosh, Amanda, go read the prize list, why don't you?" Max said impatiently. "Look, I'm sort of busy—" Max started to say.

"I know," Amanda interrupted. "Practicing." She smiled sweetly at him.

"Yeah. Well. I have to get back to—"

"Max," Amanda cut him off again. "I would very much like to be in this gymkhana. Do you think I could?"

"Well, sure," Max mumbled. "You just have to get on a team and enter."

"But I don't know anybody to be on a team with,"

Amanda said, looking sideways at him. "Couldn't I be on your team?"

"We already have enough people," Max stated flatly. "We've been practicing together, the four of us." He gestured toward Mcgan, Chloe, and Keith.

"Why don't you find your own team and enter?" Max suggested.

Amanda looked toward the barn. "Nobody wants to be on my team," she said softly. Max thought she sounded a little sad.

"Amandaaaa! Mandeee? a voice called loudly from the barn.

"That's Mama calling me," Amanda said. She climbed down on the wrong side of the fence and stood staring at it as if she hadn't planned on it and couldn't imagine how she ended up there.

"Amanda Sloane, you get yourself up to this barn right now!" Amanda's mother appeared in the barn door. You could tell from the way she stood with her hands firmly planted on her hips that she was annoyed with Amanda. Mrs. Sloane was always annoyed about something.

Amanda studied the fence for another moment, then climbed back up and got down on the other side. "Well, I have to go," she said lightly. " 'Bye." She started up the hill toward her mother, picking her way through the lush grass is if she expected to step in something unpleasant any second.

"Thank goodness we got rid of her," Megan exclaimed.

Max preferred to have as little to do with Amanda as possible. But once again, he couldn't help feeling just a little bit sorry for her. Max had been having a tough time lately, but he'd never been the only one not wanted on a team. He could just imagine how bad that would feel.

During the rest of the week before the gymkhana, the kids practiced hard. Haley, Tyler, Scott, and Melissa had formed a team and announced that they were most certainly going to win the Olympics tickets by having the highest team score. The Short Stirrup Club was determined to beat them.

They practiced starting quickly from a standstill and going from a canter to a halt. Max and Popsicle could canter to a perfect half every time. Megan and Pixie had trouble with the halts, but they were definitely the fastest starters!

Some of the games in the gymkhana involved getting off the horse to pick up objects on the ground, so they got Sharon to teach them the running dismount. All of them learned to jump off safely while their horses were trotting or cantering.

They also had to practice vaulting to get back on after the running dismount. Vaulting was tricky, but soon they had all learned to do it, first from a standstill, then when the horse was moving. Max never would have believed he could actually jump on a trotting horse and land in the saddle without using the stirrups or a mounting block.

"Chloe, you're so good at that," Max said, watching her take a running start and leap onto Bo Peep's back as she was trotting.

"I think it's because of the airbag," Chloe laughed. "The airbag" was what they all called Bo Peep's massive neck. Chloe patted the little mare. "It sort of lifts me right up on her!"

On the day before the gymkhana, they practiced bending in and out between the poles. Keith and Penny were always the quickest at it, because they'd done it so many times in western horse shows. But Megan and Pixie were almost as fast. Pixie seemed to like it. She'd flatten her ears like a cutting horse heading off a cow and go at it, making flying changes of lead left and right at every turn, then racing back to the finish line. Once, Megan nearly ran Pixie right smack into Max and Popsicle, she was so eager to get to the finish.

"Megan! You nearly crashed into us," Max said, alarmed.

"Sorry!" she said, panting and grinning with delight at how fast she'd just ridden. "Come on, let's race to the finish line, Max! We'll have to do it in the gymkhana, anyway. I'm tired of racing by myself."

"No way," Max said nervously. Then, to cover up his fear, he added, "I'm saving it for the big day."

Max was still having the nightmare about falling with Popsicle. Every day that brought them closer to the competition brought with it more anxiety for him. Whenever he rode, he was sure he was going to have a terrible accident at any second. He hadn't smiled in days. He wished he could just fall off and get it over with.

"Come on, really race me, just once," Megan pleaded with him. "Don't you want to see what it's like?"

"You'd better be more careful." Max frowned. "If you get hurt, you won't be able to compete in the gymkhana."

"I won't get hurt." Megan tossed her head carelessly.

"Well, if you keep being so reckless, someone else might," Max scolded.

"I know what I'm doing," Megan snapped. "I still think you're just a scaredy-cat, so quit talking to me like you're Dad. Anyway, I'm not afraid to go fast. Watch this—Pixie and I have been practicing our sliding stop, and we're getting much better at it." She turned Pixie around and galloped off to the end of the ring. Then she turned and galloped back as fast as she could. Keith and Chloe watched from nearby.

Max gave her an annoyed look as she headed straight for him and Popsicle. He thought she would turn before she reached them, but, with growing alarm, he realized she wasn't going to— Pixie planted her feet and came to a sliding stop when she was just a few feet away, sending up a shower of dirt.

Popsicle had been dozing. When the dirt sprayed up from Pixie's feet and stung his rump, he woke up with a snort and scooted forward, then stopped short. Max had been resting with his feet out of the stirrups. His legs swung back, and, for the second time that summer, he ended up hanging on to a horse's neck, trying to stay on. But this time, he managed to get himself back into the saddle.

"That's it," he said to Megan. His heart was thumping from the scare he'd had. He got off Popsicle and began running up the stirrups. "Find someone else to be on your team. I'm not getting killed over a stupid old gymkhana. You guys can have your Short Stirrup Club. I don't need you." He finished loosening Popsicle's girth and headed for the gate. "I don't need any of you!"

"Oh, come on, Max. I'm sorry I spooked Popsicle," Megan said.

"Max, don't leave," Keith begged. "We really need you."

"Please don't drop out now, Max," Chloe pleaded.

"The gymkhana is tomorrow. You can't let the team down."

"Why not?" Max wanted to know. "You guys don't seem to mind letting *me* down." He glared at Keith, who hung his head. "I'm sure you'll do just fine without me."

"Fine!" Megan shouted after him as he headed for the barn. "Be that way! You big baby! Who needs you, anyway?" she added. "We'll get someone else to replace you. It shouldn't be too hard to find another CHICKEN!"

9

AT THE WORD "CHICKEN," MAX STOPPED FOR A MOMENT with his back to them. He wanted to say something just as mean to his sister, but right then he couldn't think of a comeback. Then, suddenly, he didn't even care.

He trudged up the hill leading Popsicle. He should have been angry, he knew, but actually he mostly felt relieved. He'd been so worried about falling off in the gymkhana that he had been miserable every time he got on Popsicle. Now he wouldn't have to worry about it, since he wouldn't be riding in the gymkhana. But he did feel a little guilty about leaving the others without a fourth for their team the day before the competition.

He untacked Popsicle and spent a long time brushing him. When he was finished, Popsicle's coat was as smooth and shiny as it could be. Max stroked his neck and shoulder over and over, loving the feel of the soft, warm fur over the horse's muscular frame. He knew he'd gotten Popsicle really clean, because not a speck of dirt clung to his hand, even after all that petting.

He found an apple in his tack trunk and gave it to Popsicle. The horse munched and slobbered, enjoying the treat, until Max's hands were covered with foamy apple-spit. He put Popsicle in his stall and went to the wash stall to use the hose to clean his hands.

On the way, he saw Fancy walk by with a kitten dangling from her mouth. She had moved her kittens from the hay barn, probably because it was no longer a quiet place for a mama cat and her babies. Megan and Chloe had been to see them there every day, along with some of the other kids.

Max had spent plenty of time there, too, visiting the little gray-and-white kitten that was his favorite. It was smaller than the other kittens but seemed healthy otherwise. Max could pick it up, because he'd spent so much time taming it. The other kittens were much wilder. They would spit and bite if anyone tried to pick them up.

Nobody knew where Fancy had put her kittens

this time. She just couldn't seem to decide on a spot. Every day or two, someone would see her dragging a kitten from one hiding place to another. The kittens were almost a month old now, and a big mouthful for their petite mama. She'd drag one as far as she could, then have to stop and rest. The kitten would hang motionless while in her jaws, but as soon as she put it down, it would go bounding off to play or hide somewhere. Poor Fancy never got to rest! She'd go running off after her baby and try again to drag it to her new hiding place. Max thought it was pretty funny to watch. He just hoped she wouldn't run into Earl on her home-hunting adventures.

After saying good-bye to Popsicle, Max got his bike and pedaled home. He spent the rest of the afternoon in his room, reading a book that had nothing to do with horses or riding. He wanted to forget about the whole subject for a while.

Later, he heard his sister come in. She headed straight up the stairs and stood in his doorway, waiting for him to notice her. He ignored her.

Megan sighed. "Max, please don't quit the team. We really need you. I'm sorry about today. You were right. I shouldn't be such a show-off, but I get so tired of being careful all the time. Sometimes it's fun to just take a chance and do something crazy."

Max turned a page in his book and pretended to

keep on reading. He was listening to Megan, but this time she had really hurt his feelings. He wasn't going to let her get off so easily.

She tried again. "Keith and Chloe are really hoping you'll change your mind."

Max didn't answer. He stared at the book. Slowly, he turned another page.

"Max? Please don't let us down. Think of those Olympics tickets! We've been practicing so hard, we're bound to win them, if we just stick together." She made her voice sound tempting. "You know how cool it will be when we're actually there, watching Sharon ride . . ."

Max didn't move or speak. Of course, he wanted to win the tickets to the Olympics. He wanted to go to the Olympics more than anything. But he was still hurt and angry. And most of all, he was afraid he was going to fall off Popsicle.

"Well?" Megan prompted. "Are we a team again?"

Max felt his eyes start to fill up with tears, but he wasn't about to let Megan see him cry. He had been feeling so bad for so long, he wanted someone else to feel bad for a change. He opened his eyes wide, willing himself not to blink. He thought of the meanest thing he could say to his sister. Then he put down the book and looked at Megan.

"You don't need me on your team, remember?" he said quietly. "I'm just a big chicken. Why don't you ask Amanda to be on your team? She rides about as *professionally* as you." Max emphasized the word *professionally* so that it was clearly an insult. "Professional" was not exactly the word that would come to mind when describing Amanda's riding.

"Oh!" Megan exclaimed furiously.

Max stared coldly at his sister. He knew he'd made her really angry, and he was glad. Megan couldn't stand Amanda. And she'd really hate for anyone to compare her riding to Amanda's.

Megan glared back at him. "Maybe I will," she said icily. She crossed her arms, turned on her heel, and stomped into her room, closing the door hard.

Max picked up his book and held it before his face again, but he still wasn't reading. He was hiding. He had held back the tears as long as he could. Now he felt them sliding down both sides of his face and splashing onto his pillow. Some of them ran into his ears, but he didn't wipe them away. He just let them fall until there weren't anymore

The next day was Saturday, the day of the gymkhana. Megan asked her father to drive her to the barn early. Max announced he was riding his bike.

"But, Max, I'm driving anyway," his father said, looking puzzled. "Why don't you come along with us? You can throw your bike in the back of the Bronco if you want and ride it home."

"I just feel like riding my bike," Max told his dad.

"Is something going on between the two of you?" James Morrison said to his children. "You both seem awfully quiet."

"Everything's fine, Dad," Megan said.

"I just want to ride my bike," Max said again.

"Okay, suit yourself. Come on, Megan," their father said, opening the door.

Max watched the Bronco until it turned the corner and he couldn't see it anymore. Then he put on his helmet, got his bike, and coasted down the driveway. He rode down the quiet country highway that would take him to the farm, listening to his bike tires hum on the pavement. He was thinking how he'd always been busy competing in horse shows. It might be interesting to be just a spectator for a change.

He met his father at the entrance to Thistle Ridge. His dad waved at him, then headed home. Max gave him a thumps-up and pedaled up the long driveway. On the way up, he looked to see if the foals were turned out, but they weren't. Max supposed they had been put in one of the back paddocks with the mares. There would be lots of people and horses around today, and Sharon didn't like her mares and foals to be around all the hustle and bustle of a show. Max thought he could go and sec them in a little while, if he felt like it. After all, he wasn't showing today.

He went through the barn, stopping to say hello to Quasar on the way. Amanda had Prince Charming on cross-ties in the aisle. She was brushing him as if she were afraid to get too close to him. When the horse stomped at a fly, she jumped and dropped the brush. It bounced and landed at Max's feet. He picked it up and handed it to her.

"Thanks, Max," Amanda said, giving him one of her fake smiles.

"You're welcome."

"Max," Amanda began, "I'm so happy to be on a team in this gymkhana! I just think this is going to be so much fun!" She said "so. much. fun!" with a period after each word, the same way her mother sometimes talked. "I was so thrilled when your sister asked me to be on the team." Amanda beamed at him, then cringed as Prince Charming stomped again.

Max almost smiled thinking of how hard it must have been for Megan to ask Amanda to replace him. But then Amanda said something that turned his smile into a frown.

"It was just so thoughtful of you to offer to drop out and let me take your place. You are just the sweetest thing." She smiled grandly at him.

Max backed up, in case she was thinking about kissing him again. "I didn't give up my place just so you could be on the team! Max protested.

"Oh, really?" Amanda said. It was her turn to frown. "Well, that's not what your sister told me. Why did you quit?" She waited politely for him to answer.

"I dropped out because—because . . ." He faltered. He couldn't tel Amanda the real reason he had quit the team. It was too embarrassing. He scowled. Once again, his sister had gotten the better of him. "I . . . guess I did."

"Oh, I knew it!" Amanda sounded pleased. "I just knew you were a nice boy, even if you are a Yankee. I told my mother that, and even she agreed. We've always said that about you."

Max backed up even further at that thought. He was alarmed that he had been the subject of a conversation at the Sloanes' house. He turned abruptly and hurried to Popsicle's stall, nearly running into Megan on the way. They stopped and stared angrily at each other, then each went on in opposite directions.

Megan was running around like she usually did before a horse show, trying to get Pixie ready. Max sat on his tack trunk and just watched, enjoying not being part of the hectic preshow preparations for a change. Keith was also there, getting Penny ready. Max wasn't sure if Keith seemed mad. The boys avoided looking at each other.

Soon Jake Wyndham's voice came over the loudspeaker, announcing that it was time for the gymkhana to begin. Max followed Chloe, Keith, and Megan down to the arena and found a spot near the rail where he would have a good view.

There was a big poster near the in gate that listed the events in order. There was also a poster that listed the order in which the teams would compete in each event. Max scanned the list of entrants. To qualify for the high-point team award and win the Olympics tickets, each team had to enter all eight events. As far as Max could tell, there would be five teams in the running for the tickets.

The gymkhana began with the sack race. The competitors had to race, on horseback, from the starting line to the far end of the arena. There they dismounted and got into a burlap sack. Then they had to hop back, leading their horses and ponies. There were several sections of that class, since even the smaller children could compete in it.

The next event was the flag race. There were two bright orange traffic cones, one in the center of the ring containing three flags and one at the far end. The first rider on each team had to race to the far cone with a flag and put it into the cone, then pick up a flag from the second cone and hand it off to the second rider on the team, who did the same. The last rider on the team had to cross the finish line carrying the last flag. All of this had to be done without dropping a flag or knocking over a cone.

Max thought that the race was exciting to watch. Amanda started for the Short Stirrup team. She had trouble steering Prince Charming in a straight line without a rail on one side to guide her, so she put them in last place right away. Max could see Megan watching impatiently from the starting line. He chuckled to himself. Megan went last for their team and managed to make up the time that Amanda had lost. She ended up crossing the finish line a good lap ahead of the last riders on the other teams. Megan and Chloe high-fived each other and the other members of their team. Max saw Megan look at him and then look away. He didn't care. The next race was starting.

The next event was a dress-up race. The riders had to race to the end of the ring, where there was a pile of old clothing. Each rider had to dismount and put on a hat, a shirt or jacket, a pair of pants, and a pair of shoes. It was really comical watching them hobble back, leading their baffled ponies. One rider's pants kept falling down and tripping her. Another rider's horse kept trying to eat her hat! The spectators enjoyed this race even more than the competitors. By the time it was over, everybody was laughing so hard nobody really cared who had won.

The next race was called run 'n' ride. Everyone had to have a partner for this race, with one horse for each pair of riders. At the starting whistle, one person ran and the other rode to the end of the arena. A handler took the horse from the rider, who then had to run back to the finish. The handler held the horse until the other runner arrived, then the runner mounted up and galloped to the finish line. This race was easy for the horses but hard work for the riders, Max thought. The big kids' team ended up winning that event. They just had bigger horses and longer legs.

The next event didn't require much skill but, like the dress-up race, was very funny to watch. Several buckets of ice had been arranged in a circle in the center of the arena. All the riders trotted around while music played over the loudspeaker. When the music stopped, they had to get to a bucket as fast as they could without letting go of their mounts and sit down in a bucket. Riders who didn't make it to a bucket or who let go of their horses were out of the game. After each round, a bucket was removed. Max laughed out loud when two competitors raced for the same bucket, then hesitated to sit down because the ice was so cold.

Megan and another girl were the last two riders

left, with one bucket of ice. They were asked to canter around, to make it more interesting. When the music stopped, they both galloped for the bucket. The other girl dismounted and ran the last few steps to the bucket. Megan, always looking for a shortcut, just jumped off Pixie and landed seat first into the bucket with an icy splash. The other girl, who had almost reached the bucket, ended up sitting in Megan's lap. Everyone laughed for a long time at the two of them. Megan and the girl laughed the hardest.

After that, Max went to check the team standings. There were only three more events left in the gymkhana. The two teams from Thistle Ridge were neck-and-neck, with Haley and Tyler's team a few points ahead of Megan, Keith, Chloe, and Amanda. On his way back to the ringside, Max heard Megan talking to her team.

"Okay, you guys, this is our big chance! The obstacle course is next, then the drum race, then the bending race. I think we can beat the big kids in the obstacles, because our horses and ponies are littler and quicker. But we'll have to really try to go for speed, okay?"

Keith, Chloe, and Amanda all nodded. "Okay!" Megan said. "Come on, put your hands in." She stuck out her hand. Keith and Chloe hesitated, then put their hands in. Max caught Keith's eye for a minute, then he looked away. Max felt a little stab of sadness when he realized they were going to cheer for the Short Stirrup Club without him.

Tyler and Haley rode by with Scott and Melissa right behind them. Max thought they looked big and strong and fast. He saw Megan looking at the group doubtfully and knew she was thinking the same thing.

"Hey you wimps," Tyler jeered at them. "We're going to kick your little butts, right, team?"

"Right!" Haley, Melissa, and Scott said. "You can just forget about those Olympics tickets," Tyler went on.

Then Max saw Megan's face take on a determined look that he knew very well. When she looked like that, nothing had better get in her way. She glared at Tyler.

"Short Stirrup Club!" Megan and Chloe and Keith cheered. Amanda had her hand in, but she didn't say anything. Max found himself murmuring the cheer along with them, wishing that someone would beat the big kids. He hoped it would be the Short Stirrup Club.

The obstacle course began. It was fun and challenging, requiring the riders to steer around and over things, move objects from one place to another, mount and dismount, and make precise transitions from canter or trot to halt. Each rider was timed, and the time was announced after they completed the course. Near the end, when almost everyone had gone, Tyler made an amazing turn after negotiating one obstacle to get to the last one before the finish line. The rider had to ride past a jump, drop a ball into a bucket, then turn around and go over the jump. Most people had been making a circle to get an approach to the jump, which took extra time. Tyler dropped the ball into the bucket expertly, without even slowing down, then spun his horse, Rocket, right around on his haunches, putting him just two strides from the jump before the finish. It was a daring maneuver, one that required skill from both horse and rider. The crowd cheered and whistled for him as he thundered past the finish cone.

"Thirty-two twenty-nine!" Jake announced the time it had taken Tyler to finish the course. "That's the time to beat, folks."

Two more riders had to go. Their times were nowhere near that fast. Then it was Megan's turn. She made it through the first part of the course quickly. Pixie's small body turned agilely, saving time in the turns where the bigger horses had to slow down. Megan would have to make up time in the straight lines, though, Max knew, to keep up with the bigger strides of the horses. Megan picked up the ball, vaulted on Pixie, and headed for the bucket at a dead run. Suddenly, Max realized what she was going to do. She was going to try the same move Tyler had performed!

Max felt a chill of fear creep down his spine. Pixie wasn't good at halting quickly. In order to make that turn on the haunch, she would have to almost sit Pixie down and spin her around. It was a tricky move, even for a more experienced rider. Megan just didn't have the "brakes" to get Pixie to do that.

Megan reached the bucket. She threw the ball in. Max saw her lean back to try to stop Pixie and turn at the same time. Pixie only slowed down, then tried to turn sharply to obey Megan's command.

"Megan, no!" Max yelled.

But it was too late. Pixie's legs slid out from under her, and she fell right on top of Megan. The crowd gasped. Max was through the fence in an instant and running to his sister's side. Sharon got there before he was halfway down the arena and knelt down next to Megan. Pixie scrambled up and trotted, then cantered toward the in-gate.

"Loose horse!" he heard someone call out.

"I got her," someone else said.

Max reached his sister and knelt down beside Sharon.

Megan still lay where she had fallen. She hadn't moved at all.

"Megan," Max said. "Megan, are you all right?"

But his sister didn't answer him and her eyes stayed closed.

10

MAX WAS HORRIFIED. HE WANTED TO HOLD ONE OF HIS sister's hands, but he couldn't move. Sharon was bending over Megan, speaking into the walkie-talkie that she carried around at shows.

"Jake, send the EMT guys over here, quick," she was saying.

Max kept staring at his sister. Her face was ashen. Her closed eyelids were gray. He wasn't even sure she was breathing. She lay like an old rag doll somebody had carelessly dropped.

"Is she okay?" Max could barely whisper.

Sharon squeezed Max's hand and put an arm around him. "I don't know what's wrong with her," she said calmly. "But she is breathing. I think she may have hit her head. We'll just have to let the EMT guys check her out."

A few seconds later, the paramedics arrived and began checking Megan's vital signs. She began to stir, then opened her eyes.

"Wow!" she said. "Did I fall?" She squinted. "Boy, does my head hurt."

She tried to sit up, but the paramedics wouldn't let her. One of them checked her pupils and said, "Looks like she might have a concussion."

Max felt relieved that his sister was talking. She said nothing hurt except her head. Sharon wanted her to go to the hospital, but Megan refused. She said she was fine. She started to stand up, then sat down again, holding her head. Then she threw up.

"Oh, no," she said weakly. "I really hate to throw up."

"Megan, you're going to have to go to the hospital and let them check you out," Sharon said. "I've already had Jake call your mom. I'll go with you," Sharon reassured her.

Megan looked scared as the paramedics put her on the stretcher and loaded her into the ambulance. Before they closed the door, she grabbed Max's hand. "Max, please! You have to take my place in the gymkhana, okay? Please?"

Max didn't answer her. Megan looked pale and

pathetic lying on the stretcher. Max watched the ambulance drive away.

Keith and Chloe were right beside him when he turned around. "Is Megan going to be okay?" Keith asked anxiously.

"She probably just has a concussion," Max told them.

Chloe's green eyes were full of tears. "Oh, I hope she'll be okay. Poor Megan."

"Poor Megan!" Max said angrily. "I told her about a hundred times she was going to get hurt riding so recklessly. Maybe now she'll be more careful."

Then Tyler rode up on Rocket. "Yeah, it looks likc your sister just got too big for her breeches, huh?" Tyler said. "I guess you babies will just have to kiss those Olympics tickets good-bye—oh, but I forgot. You're good at kissing, right, Romeo?" Tyler made loud smooching sounds in the air.

Max felt his ears turn hot. "Just shut up, Tyler!" Max yelled at the older boy. "My sister could ride circles around you any ol' day! And so could I! So could any of us!" Max gestured to include Chloe, Keith, and Amanda.

"Well, then, why don't you, little dude? I noticed you haven't done any riding all day. Why don't you replace your sister, so we can beat your little club fair and square? In fact, I'll even tie one hand behind my back. Or are you too *chicken?*" Tyler taunted. He rode off toward the other three members of his team, flapping his elbows and clucking.

Max watched Tyler trotting away on Rocket. He knew Tyler would torture him endlessly, unless he could somehow get the best of him. Then Max knew what he could do. If the Short Stirrup Club could beat the older kids and win the Olympics tickets, they would be the big shots of the barn for a change. If Max and the younger kids proved that they could outride the big kids, Tyler would have to let up on the teasing.

"I guess Megan will be sorry when we don't win those Olympics tickets," Keith observed. "She really wanted us to beat Tyler's team."

"So, what are we waiting for?" Max said. "Let's beat them."

"How can we? Our team can't get points in the last two events without Megan. We may as well hang it up right now." Chloe sounded forlorn.

"You don't have Megan." Max sighed.

"So we lose," Keith said dejectedly.

"But you have me," Max said with determination.

"You?" Keith looked up. "But I thought you didn't want to be on our team anymore, because of how I told Haley on you and Megan called you a chicken."

"Well, I didn't," Max said. "But I guess you need me after all. I miss the Short Stirrup Club. And besides, I would just love to beat Tyler's team, especially after what he did to me!"

"Hooray!" Chloe cheered. "Max is on our team!"

"Hurry up and get your helmet and stuff," Keith told him. "There're only two more events left."

Max went to the barn, got his helmet, and put on his chaps. He quickly tacked up Popsicle and led him down to the arena. The next event was about to begin.

The drum race consisted of three jumps each made out of three old oil drums cut in half and laid end-to-end. Each rider jumped around the course. Every rider who made it around without touching a drum qualified for the second round. In the second round, one drum was removed from each obstacle. By the third round, each jump was made up of only one drum. It took a skilled rider to guide a horse successfully over such a narrow obstacle.

When it was Max's turn to go, he picked up the reins. His hands were shaking with a mixture of fear and determination as he started the course. Many of the other riders had been eliminated when their horses refused or ran around the drums instead of jumping over them. They weren't high, but they were solid.

Max gritted his teeth and kept riding, hoping Popsicle wouldn't feel how nervous he was. When the event was over, Max had made it around all three times without even touching any of the oil drums. He was the only rider who had. Everyone cheered for him as he was given the blue ribbon, but he didn't feel very happy. He was worried about Megan, and as soon as he'd mounted up, his fear of falling had come back worse than ever. It was taking all his courage to keep on competing.

The last event was a bending race. One rider zig-zagged in and out of a row of poles to his or her partner, who was waiting at the end of the row. Then they joined hands and came bending back through them to the finish. There was just enough room for the two horses between the poles. If the riders broke their grasp, they had to return to the first pole and start again.

Either Keith or Max would have to be Amanda's partner, since Chloe's pony, Bo Peep, was just too short to be paired with Prince Charming.

"I'll do it," Keith volunteered, But when they tried to join hands to practice, Penny attacked Prince Charming with her teeth! Amanda squealed and begged Keith to get away from her.

"I guess Penny doesn't like Prince," Keith said. "You'll have to do it, Max."

Max felt his stomach churn. He didn't even want to be riding. The last thing he wanted was to hold hands with Amanda Sloane in front of everybody. They would never stop teasing him about it.

But it was the last event. Their team was neck-and-neck with Tyler's team for first place. Max had already made it through the drum race without falling off. There weren't even any jumps in this event. If he could just get through this last class, it would all be over. Max made up his mind to try.

When it was his turn to go, he started off bending through the poles. Amanda was waiting for him at the end. He hesitated for a second, then locked hands firmly with her. "Let's go," he said to her.

They each had to steer with the reins in one hand, since they were holding hands. Max had made sure they tied their reins up short so that it would be easier to steer with one hand, but he knew Amanda wouldn't be very good at it—she had trouble steering with both reins. Could they make it through all the poles, then gallop to the finish without breaking their grasp?

Max's stomach felt like a hundred squirrels were crawling around in it as they started back through the poles. But luck was with them. Prince Charming was a doggy sort of horse who liked to follow other horses. And Popsicle was a good-natured gelding who didn't mind company. The two horses trotted abreast, bending in and out of the poles as if they'd done it together all their lives. When they came through the last two poles Max heard everyone cheering for them. He saw Tyler and Haley come through at the same time. If he and Amanda beat them to the finish line, they'd win the Olympics tickets and beat Tyler's team. Max felt a quiet strength surge through him. He didn't know where it came from, but suddenly he knew he was going to make this race count. Max looked at Amanda. "Come on," he said calmly. "We can do it."

Then Max did something he'd never done before, and never believed he would do. They were fifty feet from the finish line. He pressed his legs into Popsicle's sides and clucked at him, bending forward at the same time. Popsicle cantered off toward the finish line. Max urged him on. He felt Popsicle double his strides. Max knew he was going pretty fast. He also knew Popsicle could go faster. He glanced over at Haley and Tyler. Haley's thoroughbred mare, Cinnamon, was galloping hard, with Tyler's horse right beside her. They were just a little ahead of Max and Amanda. Max didn't think about falling off. He just thought about galloping his horse through the pasture. Max closed his legs on Popsicle's sides and felt the wind push his eyes nearly closed as he *let him go.*

Popsicle dug in and easily passed the other two horses, with Prince Charming right beside him. Max let go of Amanda's hand when they crossed the finish line. He was panting and grinning hugely. Everyone was cheering. Max had done it!

He had helped win the team competition for the Short Stirrup Club. In a moment, Jake announced the winners on the loudspeaker. He also announced that he'd spoken to the hospital, and Megan was going to be fine.

Max got Popsicle to slow down and then to walk. He patted him on the neck. Popsicle snorted several times. He seemed to be as pleased with himself as Max was.

"That was *great!*" Max admitted. He couldn't remember the last time he'd been so happy.

Jake came over and presented the Olympics tickets to each team member. Max accepted his, then realized that there were only four tickets. His heart sank. His ticket rightfully belonged to Megan. After all that, he still wasn't going to the Olympics.

He noticed Amanda looking at him. After a moment, she rode over and stood beside him. "Here," she said, holding out her ticket.

Max was puzzled. Why would Amanda give him her ticket?

"Take it, please," she said. "I want you to have it. I know there are only four tickets. That means Megan won't have one, or you won't. Y'all practiced so hard to win these. You take it." She put the ticket into his hand.

"But then you won't have a ticket," Max said.

"Oh, yes, I will," Amanda said. "My daddy will take me to the Olympics whenever I want." Now that her mysterious fit of generosity was over, Amanda sounded just as snobby as ever.

Max smiled. "Thanks, Amanda." He felt his happy mood begin to come back. He had overcome his fear and managed to help the Short Stirrup Club win the Olympics tickets. Tyler couldn't tease him anymore, now that Max had outridden him. He had made it through the day without falling off, though Megan hadn't. And he had finally let his horse go all out, and actually enjoyed it. Things were looking up.

He tucked the tickets into his hip pocket and walked Popsicle forward to get away from a fly that had been bothering the horse. He stopped near a jump, a wooden box that had been painted to look like a stone wall. Grayish clouds had blown in, dimming the sunlight. It looked like they might get an afternoon thundershower.

Max suddenly felt that now-familiar uneasy feeling return. Something wasn't right. What was it? He looked around and realized with a chill that he was in the exact setting of his dream.

He felt his heart begin to race. His hands trembled. The panicky feeling from his dream came over him, almost paralyzing him. He saw Sharon coming toward him. She was saying something, just like in his dream, but he couldn't understand her; she was too far away. Then he saw Earl dashing toward him as fast as the little dog's legs could carry him. Where was Earl going? He never ran like that unless he was after Fancy.

Then Max saw Fancy's little brindle head appear from under one end of the stone wall. In her jaws, she carried the gray spotted kitten that was Max's favorite. Earl jumped right between Popsicle's legs to get at her. Fancy let go of the kitten and went at Earl. Popsicle spooked at the sudden ruckus and jumped sideways. Before he even knew what had happened, Max had landed flat on his back. With the reins still in his hand, he looked up at the sky, stunned, but unharmed.

Sharon ran to his side, followed by Keith and Chloe. "Max! Are you okay?"

Max lay on his back, looking up at Sharon's face as she bent over him. Then he noticed Popsicle, also looking down at him. Popsicle seemed puzzled. He had never seen Max in this position. As the truth hit him, Max began to laugh. He had finally fallen off! It was just like he had dreamed it, though now he didn't know why the dream had seemed like such a big deal. Falling off wasn't bad at all. In fact, it was the easiest thing he'd done all day! Max sat up and looked at Sharon, who was kneeling next to him."Why are you laughing?"

Sharon said anxiously. "You didn't hit your head, did you?"

Max shook his head. He was laughing too hard to answer. Finally, he managed to say, "I never fell off a horse before! This is my first fall!"

"Never?" Sharon looked incredulous.

"I've been so worried about it, lately," Max explained. "I couldn't even enjoy riding because of it. And I was having this dream . . ." He began to laugh again. "I dreamed my fall! Not exactly like this, but almost. I'm so relieved."

"Max, everyone falls off," Sharon said. "It's inevitable. Do you know how many times I've fallen? Countless. And did you know that there's an old saying among people who ride horses? Everyone must fall off three times before they can become a really good rider."

"Then I should be an expert by now," Keith observed.

Everyone laughed. Chloe had managed to catch Earl. She held him firmly under one arm while he kept growling at Fancy. Fancy stalked away, switching her tail, to look for yet another home for her babies.

"Well, at least now I won't dread the other two falls," Max said.

He noticed the kitten peeking out from behind the stone wall where Fancy had dropped him. Max scooped up the kitten, who looked up at him curiously. "Thanks, kitty," he said, smiling.

The kitten curled itself into a contented ball and began to purr.

"Come on, let's get in the barn before it rains," Sharon said, helping Max to his feet.

Max got up and took Popsicle's reins. The heavy feeling he'd been carrying around inside was completely gone. He felt in his pocket for the tickets. Already, he was dreaming of seeing Sharon ride in the Olympics. And he was even looking forward to falling off again! He cradled the kitten his arms and headed up to the main barn. More adventures were waiting at Thistle Ridge. And Max couldn't wait to be a part of them.

About the Author

ALLISON ESTES grew up in Oxford, Mississippi. She wrote, bound, and illustrated her first book when she was five years old, learned to drive her grandfather's truck when she was eight, and got her first pony when she was ten. She has been writing, driving trucks, and riding horses ever since.

Allison is a trainer at Claremont Riding Academy, the only riding stable in New York City. She currently lives in Manhattan with her seven-year-old daughter, Megan, who spends every spare moment around, under, or on horses.

SADDLE UP FOR MORE ADVENTURES WITH MEGAN, MAX, CHLOE, KEITH, AND AMANDA IN

SHORT STIRRUP CLUB™ #4

WINNER'S CIRCLE
(Coming in mid-August 1996)

Megan and her pony, Pixie, have always been a great team, and they've been working hard with their trainer, Sharon Wyndham, to get ready for a big horse show. But trouble begins when Megan and Max's grandmother comes for a visit. Nana Morrison believes Megan has what it takes to be a champion—but not with Pixie!

Then Megan suddenly gets the chance to ride Amanda Sloane's flashy horse, Prince Charming, in the horse show. Now Megan must decide between impressing her grandmother or sticking up for the pony she loves.

STORIES FOR EVERY HORSE LOVER

By Anne Eliot Crompton

The Snow Pony

Janet is new in town, and has no friends. Then she gets a job caring for a wild pony. But when it's time for the pony to be given away, will Janet be alone again? Or has she learned how to make friends and keep them?

The Rainbow Pony

Alice and Jinny are best friends, but Jinny is very bossy, and Alice doesn't like to fight. Then one day Alice rescues a pony, but her father has a "no animals" rule so she secretly keeps it at Jinny's place. Soon Alice will have to take care of the pony herself—even if it means standing up to her dad and Jinny, too.

The Wildflower Pony

The sequel to *The Rainbow Pony*

Alice's pony surprises her by giving birth to a foal. How can she ever afford to feed *two* ponies? Then she hears about the Fourth of July contest. The best animal act will be awarded $500. With two adorable ponies and lots of practice, Alice is sure she can win. But if she doesn't, will she still be able to keep the foal?

Published by Pocket Books

1234